"This Could Be Our Chance!"

Regan cried. "Our *only* chance of getting out of here alive!"

"Regan, I told you we'll get out of here, and we will!" Adam promised.

"I don't believe you!" she said in despair.

He gazed at her. There were tears welling at the corners of her eyes. The sight of them stirred something in him that was both protective and possessive, a warm, liquid, male yearning in the pit of his stomach.

"I know you're scared," he told her, his voice soft and husky. "But I promise you, Regan, I won't let anything happen to you. We will survive, and we will get out."

"I know," she whispered. "I—I trust you."

Reason vanished. Self-control vanished. His body sank over hers until he was fully covering her length. His mouth settled urgently against hers as he took her in a deep, searing kiss.

Dear Reader:

Welcome to Silhouette Desire – provocative, compelling, contemporary love stories written by and for today's woman. These are stories to treasure.

Each and every Silhouette Desire is a wonderful romance in which the emotional and the sensual go hand in hand. When you open a Desire, you enter a whole new world – a world that has, naturally, a perfect hero just waiting to whisk you away! A Silhouette Desire can be light-hearted or serious, but it will always be satisfying.

We hope you enjoy this Silhouette today – and will go on to enjoy many more.

Please write to us:

Jane Nicholls
Silhouette Books
PO Box 236
Thornton Road
Croydon
Surrey
CR9 3RU

JEAN
BARRETT
HELD HOSTAGE

Silhouette Desire

Originally Published by Silhouette Books
a division of
Harlequin Enterprises Ltd.

*First published in Great Britain in 1993
by Silhouette Books, Eton House, 18-24 Paradise Road,
Richmond, Surrey TW9 1SR*

© R. L. Rogers 1992

*Silhouette, Silhouette Desire and Colophon are
Trade Marks of Harlequin Enterprises B.V.*

ISBN 0 373 58741 4

22-9302

Made and printed in Great Britain

JEAN BARRETT

was a teacher for many years and now writes full-time.
Jean and her spouse live in a Chicago suburb for nine
months of the year. Summers are spent on Wisconsin's
Door Peninsula, where the couple walk the woods and
shore, collect country antiques and try to deal as polite-
ly as possible with the annual chipmunk invasion.

Jean keeps her readers very much in mind when she
writes her books. "The stories are for them," she says.
"If I can please them with what I write, then I've done
my job."

Other Silhouette Books by Jean Barrett

Silhouette Desire

Hot on Her Trail
Heat
A Ring of Gold

To the gang,
Mitzi and Jerry, Priscilla and Richard,
Sharon and Jim, Beth,
Gloria, Nancy and Peg,
with every affection

One

Regan MacLeod glanced at her wristwatch and frowned. She couldn't understand what was keeping the bush pilot. He had promised her they would leave exactly at nine this morning, and it was already twenty minutes past the hour. It was a long flight to Thompson, and she couldn't afford to miss her commercial connection to Minnesota. Besides, she was eager to get away from this place. Guilt, she supposed, a sense of failure before she had even begun.

Wishing she could convince herself she wasn't running away from anything, that she was only going home, Regan stirred restlessly on the hard wooden bench. She hoped the delay with the plane wasn't anything serious like an engine problem or a forecast of bad weather. There was no one she could ask. The pilot was somewhere out on the field, and she was alone in the small waiting room.

The building was more shack than air terminal. But its rough board walls had been brightened with a series of the quilted and embroidered hangings that were a specialty of the area. They were the colorful, artistic product of the local women. Like the soapstone carvings created by the Inuit men in a dusty glass case beside the door, they were for sale to the occasional visitors who traveled to this isolated community. Regan, admiring them, was sorry she couldn't be as enthusiastic about everything else in the settlement.

Her gaze wandered to the calendar tacked above the glass case. It was two years old and tattered. She could only guess it was kept there because its scene of a tropical beach reminded someone that there were places where palm trees dipped in the trade winds and a travel-poster sun shone warmly every day. At this latitude, even though it was April, the barren terrain was still wrapped in winter.

She smiled wryly at the calendar, remembering that many of her fellow teachers had been headed for similar beaches in Florida and the Bahamas. They had been disbelieving when they had heard her own plans for the spring vacation.

"A wilderness outpost on the rim of Hudson Bay! Regan, that's the wrong direction!"

They had thought her even crazier when she'd confided she was considering a teaching job for next year in the remote settlement she was visiting. So had her family.

Her brother, Joe, had grinned at her in that aggravating way. "You're kidding, right? I mean, Reg, you're the girl who's too timid to drive alone into downtown Minneapolis."

Her sister, Dru, had raised a disapproving eyebrow. "Reggie, *why?* This isn't you."

Her parents had been slightly more tactful on the subject, her father asking gently, "Honey, are you actually serious about this?"

Well, of course, she was serious. And not without good reason, either. She was twenty-seven years old, and it was time she made a change in her life. She needed an existence more stimulating than the placid St. Paul suburb where she had been working with third-graders for the past four years. She had a longing to make a difference in people's lives, to be useful in an exceptional sense. Having read about Inuit children and their needs, she'd been convinced she could achieve that intention here in Frazer Inlet.

If it hadn't been for Keith Spencer, however, she might never have acted on her aim. She and Keith had dated regularly, but the relationship had cooled last winter when Regan realized how badly her grassroots values clashed with his corporate ambitions. For one thing, he had wanted her to invest her savings in one of his schemes, and she'd been afraid of the risk. Mistaken though Keith had been, he had done her a favor in their final parting when he had said, "Face it, Regan, you're a wimp scared of the adventures life has to offer you."

Damn it, she wasn't a wimp! It wasn't supposed to be that way! Not with her heritage! From her Highland forefathers she had a mane of russet hair that tumbled to her shoulders, a pair of animated sherry-colored eyes that had the quality of smiling even when the rest of her features were in repose, and a stubborn chin on a face that was generally regarded as attractive. All these things were meant to add up to the spirit and courage that had compelled her immigrant Scottish ancestors to tackle the Manitoba prairies over a century ago.

In the end, it was mostly sheer stubbornness, the need to prove Keith and everyone else wrong, that had recklessly brought her to Frazer Inlet. The local school committee here had promptly assured her of a teaching job for next fall.

"They're in the process of opening up a new oil field near here," she had been told. "It will mean more families and more classrooms. And having been born and educated in Canada, you're certainly qualified."

Regan should have been excited about their confidence in her. But faced with the reality of Frazer Inlet—the rigorous climate, the primitive living conditions, the culture so drastically different to her own—her resolve had failed her in the long week she had spent on this desolate, rocky coastline. She had informed the school committee that she would seriously consider their offer. Inwardly she was convinced she wasn't tough enough for the job. So here she was, flying back to her dull suburb where she was going to be completely safe, and probably enormously bored, for the rest of her life. She could already hear the smug reactions of people like Keith Spencer. It was very depressing.

Feeling that she was letting herself down, but unable to see what she could do about it, Regan shifted again on the bench. She reminded herself with another glance at her watch that the pilot had yet to put in an appearance. What was the holdup? Just who or what were they waiting for?

She was beginning to get really worried, thinking about bundling herself in her parka and going out on the all-weather field to look for him, when the door opened. Icy currents of outside air that the room's inadequate oil stove struggled to combat rushed in with the pilot.

He crossed to her, a stocky man with a round face and a dark fringe of hair indicating his Inuit bloodlines. She was surprised by his expression. She had found him to be a jovial man on the flight up from Thompson. Now he looked solemn and faintly uneasy.

"Sorry you were kept waiting all this time, Ms. Mac-Leod."

"Is there a problem, John?"

He nodded unhappily. "I'm afraid there is. It's, uh, kind of a tricky situation. I was just told I have to carry two other passengers, and they have to go out on this flight. Official business. No choice about it."

She gazed up at him from the bench, perplexed. "But why should that be a problem? There's plenty of room on the plane, isn't there?"

"Yes, but this is a special case. The circumstances are, well, sensitive."

"I don't understand."

"They don't want any other passengers on board. They don't think it would be a good idea."

Regan was frustrated by his failure to clearly explain. "Are you telling me I can't take this flight?"

He looked increasingly uncomfortable. "I feel bad about it, Ms. MacLeod. I know you've already paid for the return and booked the flight, but they're asking you to wait for the next plane out day after tomorrow."

She shook her head vigorously. "I'm sorry, but that's just impossible. I have to leave now, or I won't be there when school resumes on Monday." Besides, she didn't want to linger here and be reminded of her defeat.

He grunted sympathetically. "All right, I'll go talk to them again. I'll see what I can do."

Regan waited until the door closed behind him, and then she left the bench and flew over to the window overlooking the airfield. What was this all about anyway?

The glass was frosted with ice, but through one clear corner she could see John approaching a heavy-duty vehicle parked near the terminal. There was a uniformed officer wearing a fur cap and leaning against the driver's door. She recognized his RCMP insignia.

John spoke to him, and then the Mountie rapped on a rear window of the vehicle. The window was lowered. At this distance Regan couldn't see the occupants of the back seat, but she watched the pilot and the officer bending over to confer with whoever was inside. They seemed to be arguing earnestly, and then the back window was abruptly raised. The Mountie went back to his post at the driver's door, and John started toward the terminal.

Regan, not wanting him to think she had been spying, left the window and returned to her seat on the bench. She waited hopefully and was rewarded with a cheerful grin on the pilot's face when he clomped back into the room.

"It's all set," he informed her. "You can join the flight."

"That's a relief. I appreciate your running interference for me, John." She got to her feet, smoothing down the bottom of her cream-colored turtleneck sweater. She was wearing the sweater under an open blue denim jacket of a matching slacks outfit that suited her trim, coltish figure.

She was reaching for her tote and camera bag when the pilot warned her, "Uh, there's just one thing, Ms. Mac-Leod."

"What's that?"

"You can take the flight all right, but they're asking you not to communicate in any way with the two men flying with us."

She stared at him, more mystified than ever.

"I know this is all a bit funny," he added hastily, "but it's a question of security, I guess."

She nodded slowly. "All right. No questions, I promise." What was going on here?

While she slipped into her parka, the pilot picked up her suitcase, leading the way out of the terminal. The air was clear and brittle as they joined the Mountie. He nodded at her respectfully, but there were no introductions.

"We're ready," John told him.

"The lady here understands?"

"She understands," the pilot assured him.

"Okay." The Mountie knocked again on the frosted window of the car. At his signal, the back door on the opposite side opened and a slight, sandy-haired man climbed out, hauling on a topcoat over an immaculate business suit that looked out of place in Frazer Inlet.

Regan detected a southern American accent in his voice when he ducked his head, calling back into the car a sharp, "All right, Fuller, out on your side."

The door closest to Regan was opened by the Mountie. Another man appeared, stepping slowly out of the back of the vehicle. Dark hair, almost black. A square, blunt face with a strong jaw. An expression that was silent and withdrawn. Grim.

He stood there waiting, hands behind his back, looking at none of them. His erect, compact body gave the impression of a formidable height, and Regan was surprised when the Mountie shut the door and moved over close to him. The man was actually shorter by a couple of inches than the lanky, six-foot Mountie.

She had another surprise when the officer asked his charge to turn around. Shocked, she watched the Mountie as he checked a pair of handcuffs clamped to Fuller's wrists.

By this time the sandy-haired man had rounded the vehicle. He had a parka in his hand and he draped it negligently over its owner's broad shoulders. "This should do you, Fuller, while we get out to the plane."

Fuller made no comment. He acted as if he were immune to the frigid air, though the dark cords and crew-neck sweater hugging his solid body couldn't have been warm enough by themselves. It was the sandy-haired man, shivering in his topcoat, who looked as though he hated the cold as much as he resented the assignment that had brought him to this climate.

Regan was beginning to understand the situation, and she didn't care for it one bit. By all appearances, the Mountie was assisting a plainclothesman to extradite a fugitive to the States. The man called Fuller was their prisoner. She would be sharing a cramped plane with him on a long flight. She'd be a fool if this realization didn't make her apprehensive. And it did. But she had no choice about it.

The Mountie dragged a pair of suitcases out of the vehicle. Presumably they belonged to Fuller and the plainclothesman. "All right, let's go." Carrying the cases, he led the way to the six-seater Cessna standing ready out on the field. Regan and John brought up the rear with her own luggage.

At the plane they waited to board, their breaths fogging on the air, while the bush pilot stored their gear in the deep interior compartment behind the last pair of seats. None of the men spoke to Regan. They were ignoring her existence.

"Okay, Fuller," the plainclothesman instructed his prisoner as he unlocked the handcuffs. "I'm gonna cuff you in front now so you can ride comfortably under the seat belt, but no cute stuff." He behaved as though he were doing his charge the favor of being magnanimously human.

The Mountie, concern in his voice as he watched his fellow officer secure the handcuffs in a new position, asked softly, "You going to be all right taking him on your own from here?"

"Sure. I've got another man joining me in Thompson for the long haul from there." He chuckled smugly, patting the slight bulge under his coat that was obviously his service revolver. "Besides, Fuller isn't going anywhere. Are you, Fuller?"

Regan decided she didn't like the young American cop. He was being insensitive, taunting his prisoner as though he enjoyed exerting his authority over someone in a helpless position.

Flushing with indignation, she glanced at Fuller's face to learn his reaction. There was no response from him. He remained silent, though she thought she noticed his proud jaw tightening over the unnecessary gibe. He didn't meet her gaze. She turned her head quickly away. She didn't want to feel sorry for him. He was probably dangerous, maybe a hardened criminal under that clean, appealing masculinity, and her sympathy would be unwise.

John finished stowing the baggage and told them they could board. The plainclothesman settled in the second pair of seats with his prisoner beside him. Regan sat up front next to the bush pilot. Their coats were piled on the third row of seats.

"Have a safe trip," the Mountie wished them, latching the door and stepping away from the plane.

Minutes later, the Cessna was lifting smoothly toward the clear blue sky. The plane banked over the airfield before heading south, and Regan had a last glimpse of Frazer Inlet. The huddle of buildings looked very small and lonely in all that vast whiteness. She would probably never see the place again. She tried not to regret it, but she could almost feel the ghosts of her heroic Scottish ancestors being disappointed in her.

No one spoke inside the aircraft. John was busy at his controls, and the plainclothesman seated directly behind her chewed on a stick of gum and looked bored. Regan didn't trust herself to glance at the prisoner, though she was as aware of his existence as she was of the strained silence within the close cabin. She kept herself busy with the scenery outside her window.

It was hard to believe that within a matter of weeks all that forlorn, frozen tundra passing below would be alive with masses of tiny wildflowers and gushing streams. It fascinated her, though she was more interested in trying to spot a herd of caribou. It was when she twisted in her seat and turned her head, wanting to see out both sides of the plane, that her eye fell on Fuller just behind the pilot.

Against her better judgment, she permitted her gaze to linger on him. It seemed safe enough. He was paying no attention to any of them as he stared out his window, wrapped in his own dark thoughts. His profile was like chiseled stone, a slight hump in his proud nose suggesting it had been broken in the past. His face betrayed none of his feelings, except maybe for his wide mouth. There was the barest trace of a cynical smile at the corners and something that might have been vulnerability. Or was this just her imagination because she felt his bitter anger, his inner torment? And because, want to or not, she did feel sorry for him in his hopeless situation.

She couldn't help it. He intrigued her. Who was he exactly? What terrible thing had he done that had impelled a police officer to travel all the way to the far reaches of Hudson Bay to bring him back to the States in handcuffs?

Fuller sensed her gaze on him and swiveled his head. The gaze from a pair of steel-hard gray eyes collided with hers. There was a strange intimacy in his stare that was as riveting as a guilty embrace. The breath caught in Regan's throat. The impact of his long, searing look stunned her for a second. Then, stiffening, she quickly turned her head away and faced breathlessly forward in her seat.

She was a fool. Why hadn't she noticed at the very start that men like Fuller, virile, with a powerful appeal, were dangerous in a way other than criminal? She had no business thinking about him. She reminded herself again that, however respectable his appearance, he was a man in handcuffs. There had to be a good reason for that.

From then on she concentrated on nothing but the scenery out her own window, not daring to glance around again, though she was nervously conscious of the man behind her.

The tundra below began to give way to the first evidences of the boreal forests. Long fingers of spruce and fir fringed the snow-clad waterways, making a bewildering maze of the landscape.

Just before noon, the plane began to descend. John announced a midflight break at another wilderness air station where the Cessna would be refueled and his passengers could have lunch.

The station offered nothing but a snack bar with prepackaged sandwiches. Regan had had a big breakfast at the guest house in Frazer Inlet. She wasn't interested in joining the men who disappeared inside the small terminal after the plane landed. She needed to stretch her legs on the airfield. Besides, she didn't want to be in the company of the prisoner any more than was necessary.

She found an outside door to a rest room, and she used that. Then, snug in her parka and fur-lined boots, she began to walk to the far end of the field. The air was cold but pure and bracing.

Regan was excited when she neared the end of the deserted runway and discovered caribou just off the edge of the field. They were browsing contentedly on clumps of stunted willow. She knew from her school days in Winnipeg that, unlike the caribou of the open tundra who roved in great herds, these were woodland caribou who lived in small groups. But they were caribou just the same, and all this week she had been hoping to glimpse caribou in the wild.

If they were aware of her, they didn't seem to mind her presence. She was able to spend several enchanted minutes quietly observing them.

Oh, she had to have a picture of this! Her third-graders back home would be delighted when she showed them. The light was just right, and the animals didn't seem in any hurry to move on. But her camera was somewhere in the plane.

Careful not to startle them, Regan backed away slowly. When she had put a comfortable distance between herself and the caribou, she turned and sped eagerly toward the Cessna.

Inside the plane she searched for her camera bag on the third row of seats where the coats had been piled. It wasn't there. Damn! John must have stuffed it into the luggage locker with her suitcase. Praying she could find it in time to get her picture, Regan dived down behind the rear seats and began to rummage through the baggage.

It was frustrating. The compartment was narrow and deep. He must have put the camera bag in there first, and that meant it was all the way at the back, out of easy reach. Still hoping she could find it in time, she ducked her head under the low opening and crawled on hands and knees into the compartment. Squeezing past suitcases, her fingers groped for the bag.

The space was dark and smelled of stale odors. Its walls were insulated, because the plane sometimes carried perishables, so outside sound was muffled. Regan was aware of nothing but her desire to get the camera. Her hand was finally closing on the strap of the bag when, without warning, the Cessna's engine roared into life.

Her head whipped up in alarm, cracking against the roof of the locker. There was a sharp pain in her skull. And then there was nothing.

Regan found herself stretched out like a log when she came back to reality. Stunned by the blow to her head, she must have passed out. How long she had been unconscious she didn't know. Maybe for several minutes. Her hand went to the back of her skull. She could find no evidence of swelling, and nothing was aching. She did feel a little dazed still, as though the floor under her were in motion.

And then, as her mind fully cleared, she realized that the floor *was* in motion. What's more, the droning in her ears had nothing to do with the blow to her head. It was the airborne sound of the plane's engine. The Cessna was no longer on the ground.

She wasn't imagining it! They *were* in the air!

Lifting herself to her knees, Regan backed slowly out of the compartment and dragged herself to her feet. The slight roll of the plane, along with her state of shock, made her unsteady. Gripping the backs of the seats while hunched over under the low ceiling, she worked her way forward.

Her panic, that sense of something being terribly wrong, mounted as she realized that neither John nor the plainclothesman were on the plane with her. There was only one other occupant of the aircraft. He sat at the controls in the pilot's seat, offering her a view of his broad shoulders in his gray crew-neck sweater. She didn't need to see his face. She knew who he was. The man in handcuffs! But he was no longer in handcuffs, and she was alone with him three thousand feet over the Canadian wilderness!

The plane swayed, and Regan swayed with it, lightheaded with sudden fear. He must have felt her motion, sensed there was someone behind him. His head came flashing around, the expression on his face as shocked as hers as he saw her standing there.

"Oh, my God!" he growled in a voice like rough gravel. "Where did *you* come from?"

Fighting to preserve self-control, she managed to answer him with a hoarse, "I—I was in the luggage compartment."

"You were *what?*"

"I was inside the luggage compartment. The sound of the engine startled me, and I banged my head against the roof. I must have passed out for a minute."

He stared at her as though she were crazy.

"I was searching for my camera. There were caribou out on the end of the airfield. You must have seen them. I wanted to—never mind, it doesn't matter."

He went on staring at her. Obviously he had yet to believe she was on the plane with him. He must have thought he had left her back at the airfield with the others. Clinging to the back of the seat next to his in order to keep her balance, she glanced out the side of the Cessna, realizing that they were still climbing and that they must be miles from the air station.

She could see from Fuller's face that he didn't know yet just what he was going to do about her. Regan made up his mind for him. "I don't know what happened back there or how you made it happen, and right now I don't care. All I want is out of it. You're going to have to turn the plane around and take me back."

His laughter was deep and brusque. "I will, huh?"

"You have no right to include me in this—this insanity of yours. Just take me back," she demanded, "and then I don't care where you fly this plane."

His gray eyes were like frost. "Think again, sweetheart."

His callousness outraged Regan. "What you're doing constitutes kidnapping!"

"Like hell it does! I didn't ask you to this party. I had no idea anyone was back there."

"And you didn't stop to look before you stole the plane!" she countered furiously.

"Yeah, well," he informed her in a gritty drawl that, even in her agitation, she recognized as Texan, "I wasn't exactly in a position to check the cargo before I took off. I thought you were somewhere off on that walk of yours."

"I told you why I came back to the plane!" Under her fear was a rising anger that gave her just enough courage to go on challenging him, even though she realized he might be extremely dangerous. "You can't do this! You've got to take me back!"

"All I've got to do is fly this plane. And all you've got to do," he ordered her, "is to settle your bottom in this seat next to me where I can keep an eye on you. If you don't try to interfere, you've got nothing to worry about. As soon as we land again, you can get out and walk away. I won't stop you."

"Where? When?"

"Sweetheart," he warned her, "you're making me nervous."

Regan decided to obey him. He was giving her no other option. It was useless to go on arguing with him and a risk to herself when, under the circumstances, he must be very desperate. Besides, she was still feeling weak in the knees and needed to sit down. There was a bit of turbulence that had the Cessna bouncing slightly, and this didn't help, either. He seemed to be handling the plane capably enough, however. Even her sudden appearance hadn't sidetracked him in his management of the controls. Obviously this was a skill neither the bush pilot nor the plainclothesman had been aware of.

Easing herself into the seat beside him, her fingers fumbled for the seat belt. She felt sick with dread, and the memory of John and the police officer had her wondering what he had done to them to make his escape. Unwise though it might be, she couldn't resist asking him about that.

"The pilot and the man escorting you," she said tensely. "What did you do to them?"

He kept his eyes on his flying now and didn't answer her for a moment. Then he responded with a blithe, "Worried about them? Well, don't be. They're fine. Or will be," he added with a humorless smile, "when they manage to break out of that storeroom I locked them into, along with the guy tending the airfield."

"How—how did you get free?"

The wide shoulders lifted in a casual shrug. "The smart-aleck cop wasn't so smart. He made two mistakes. He removed my handcuffs so I could use the bathroom and eat, and he was careless about his gun, just asking to have it lifted off him. You can believe I didn't think twice about taking advantage of the opportunity. I guess he must have figured I had nowhere to run, even if I did make a break for it. If he'd bothered to check a background sheet on me, he would have realized I know how to fly a plane. Now you know, just in case you're planning to write a book about it when all this is over."

When all this is over. The thought made her frantic. The situation made her frantic. She had come to northern Canada for the sake of adventure, to escape a boring existence, but she had never bargained for anything like this! "You can't possibly get away with it," she argued with him desperately. "You can't expect to steal a plane and just disappear with it. You'll have to land sometime, and when you do they'll be waiting for you."

He turned his head, training those fierce gray eyes on her. "If I were you, I wouldn't be worrying about that. I'd be thinking about how I was going to make the best of the situation. Because, like it or not, you're in this with me."

Regan forgot that she had ever felt anything like sympathy for this man. All she could feel now was terror and indignation. But he was right about one thing. If she were going to survive this nightmare, she had to stay calm, tell herself that everything was going to be all right. She tried to think, to count her chances for rescue.

The bush pilot must have filed a flight plan. The plane was expected at Thompson. But Fuller wouldn't be foolish enough to land there. He must have some other destination in mind. But where? Where could he expect to go in all this wilderness? Her eye went to the plane's compass. She knew little about it, but they seemed to be on a more westerly bearing now.

Regan tried to remember her geography. In northern Manitoba there was only one other town large enough to provide him with a possible escape route. Flin Flon, and that was to the west. Were they headed for Flin Flon?

But what good would it do her to know where they were going? Unless . . .

Her eyes left the compass and went swiftly, longingly to the plane's radio. Could she possibly get the chance to call out a plea for help?

Without even turning his head, Fuller was aware of where her gaze was resting. He answered her hope with a low, lethal, "Don't even consider it."

Regan shivered over his warning. She remembered the service revolver he had lifted from the plainclothesman. There was no evidence of it on him now, but that didn't mean he didn't have it still and wouldn't—

Radio, she suddenly realized. Not this radio. A radio back at the air station. There had to be one. When the men broke out of that storeroom they'd use it, and every airfield within flying range of the Cessna would be alerted. But what if Fuller had thought of that and smashed the radio? She had to find out. She couldn't stand not knowing.

"They'll use the radio back at the air station," she told him with as much confidence as she could muster. "When they break out of the storeroom, they'll call a warning on the radio. You don't stand a chance."

He didn't bother answering her. He just smiled, a small, grim smile. Her heart sank. So, he *had* remembered the radio, and he had taken care of that, too. He had covered all the bases. It was useless then. All she could do was wait and endure and hope.

Regan briefly considered pleading with him, appealing to his conscience. But she decided the effort would be pointless. If he had gone to such reckless lengths to escape, then the crime he was accused of must be a serious one. Men like him didn't respond to their consciences, if they even had them to begin with. Fuller was probably lacking in all compassion.

"Your head," he said abruptly.

"What?"

"Your head," he repeated. "You said you banged it on the roof of the baggage locker and passed out from the blow. Are you going to be all right?"

"I—yes, I'm fine."

"Sure?"

"Yes." In fact, she didn't have so much as a headache.

He nodded, satisfied, then lapsed into silence.

His unexpected concern, just when she had convinced herself he wasn't capable of concern, was bewildering. Any quality of sensitivity seemed totally out of character for him. He confused her feelings, and she didn't like her confusion. It was easier to simply think the worst of him.

Regan huddled there, trying to control her anxiety, trying to keep her eyes from straying in his direction. But she couldn't prevent her awareness of his disarming bulk close beside her. Against her will, his unsettling nearness had her gaze drifting toward him again and again.

She kept noticing things about him she didn't want to notice: like the way his thick hair was shaggy at the back of his strongly corded neck; how the dark corduroy jeans stretched tautly over his muscled thighs; that his eyebrows were heavy and black over those cool, confident gray eyes trained on the controls. His craggy features had a healthy color, evidence of an outdoor existence. She even detected his scent, something faintly musky and robustly male.

And she hated her observations. Hated them as much as the strange little tremors chasing through her whenever she glanced his way. She blamed the tremors on her fear. This was an understandable explanation. An *acceptable* explanation. Anything else in her situation would be unthinkable.

He interrupted the silence with another abrupt question, startling her out of her tense reverie. "What's your name?"

"I—what?"

"Your name," he demanded. "Unless you want me to go on calling you sweetheart."

"It—it's Regan. Regan MacLeod."

He nodded. "I'm Fuller. Adam Fuller."

She didn't respond to that. She wasn't sure it was wise knowing anything about him that would make him less of a stranger to her.

There was another long pause, and then he asked her, "What were you doing in Frazer Inlet?"

"Does it matter?"

He shook his head. "You don't have to tell me if you don't want to."

She hesitated, then decided that it didn't make any difference. "I'm a teacher. I was visiting their school on my spring vacation, investigating the possibility of taking a job there next year to work with Inuit children."

He turned his head, glancing at her briefly. He said nothing, but she could swear there was actually a glint of admiration in his eyes. But that couldn't be possible. Not with someone like Fuller. Anyway, there wasn't anything to admire when she remembered she was a coward running away from Frazer Inlet and its demanding conditions.

But she did find sufficient courage to ask him, "And what were you doing there?"

He turned his head away with a curt, "You ask too many questions, Regan MacLeod."

There was one last question she couldn't resist, something she felt she needed an answer to. "What did they arrest you for?"

At first she didn't think Adam Fuller was going to reply. And then flatly, matter-of-factly, he told her in one chilling word. "Murder."

Two
_____

Adam regretted his disclosure the instant it was out of his mouth and he saw her face. Her features were stiff with horror, her eyes bleak with renewed fear. He hadn't meant to terrify her in that clumsy way. Lord knew, she was already scared enough by this whole mess in which he had unintentionally landed her.

Strictly speaking, his thoughtless revelation was the truth. He had been arrested for murder. Whether he was guilty of the accusation was another story, an ugly one at that. He considered tempering his hasty admission with an explanation that would ease the blow. He decided against that. He couldn't be soft about any of this, not if he was going to achieve his intention. And he was determined to do just that, whatever it cost him.

So it was better Regan MacLeod think the worst about him. That way, she'd be less likely to challenge his authority. He wanted her ready to obey his instructions without hesitation in order to minimize the risk to both of them. He meant for them to walk away from this situation without harm.

Easier said than done, he realized. Another quick glance at her informed him that the initial shock had subsided and that she was in no mood to be meekly cooperative, even with an accused murderer.

She was going to be a problem. Adam had seen that right away, had understood it on some subliminal level back there before the air station when their gazes had collided so potently. Even then, he had admired her spirit, found her disturbingly appealing.

Oh, she had a reserve of spunk all right, whether she knew it or not. A lot of women in her threatened position would be hysterical by now, not quietly, stubbornly resistant. But she was no ordinary woman. She couldn't be if she meant to go up there and teach in that godforsaken outpost that was Frazer Inlet. Maybe her grit was a Scottish legacy, like her name and that wild russet hair.

And maybe he was crazy. What difference did it make how tempting she was when he didn't trust women these days? Not after his experience. Anyway, he couldn't afford the distraction. He had to concentrate on his escape, figure out how he was going to get back across the U.S. border without being caught. All else was unimportant.

Even so, he couldn't shake his guilt that Regan was involved in this reckless flight with him. The last thing he wanted was to hurt her. He wished he could return her to the air station, but that wasn't possible. It was imperative that he use every available minute to put as much distance as he could between himself and recapture. Otherwise, he stood no chance of resuming the urgent search that had been interrupted by his arrest.

Besides, there was the matter of fuel. Taking her back would consume too much of the precious supply, and they were already flying on the auxiliary tank. He was worried about that.

Adam made the mistake right then of peering at the gauge. She caught him checking it, and her own gaze flicked over to the instrument panel. She immediately discovered the low position of the fuel indicator. Uttering a little gasp, she stared at him, forgetting all about his shocking confession as a new fear gripped her.

"Why is the needle down like that?" she demanded. "The plane was refueled at the air station, wasn't it?"

He didn't answer her.

"Tell me," she insisted.

"No," he admitted finally, "it wasn't refueled."

"But I thought—"

"Yeah, so did I until I got out to the plane and checked." He shrugged. "I guess the attendant hadn't gotten around to that little job when I put him into the storeroom. The fuel supply was locked, and I wasn't going to risk going back and searching for a key."

"So you just took off knowing—" Regan couldn't say it. She couldn't believe that anyone would be so wildly irresponsible. But, of course, that was the whole point. This man wasn't responsible, and she was trapped with him.

"Don't worry," he told her calmly. "We have just enough fuel to get us where we're going."

"Where is that? Why won't you tell me?"

"The less you know, the better off you'll be."

Infuriating! He was infuriating! But there was no point in complaints or recriminations. All she could do was wait and pray.

She kept still in the eternal half hour that followed, trying to avoid glancing at the fuel gauge. But, repeatedly, she found her gaze wandering to the indicator, watching the arrow as it steadily descended in its arc. Finally she could no longer keep silent.

"It's going down awfully fast, isn't it?"

He said nothing. She looked at him, noticing his taut expression. "Severe headwinds," he told her at last. "We've been battling them for the last half hour. It's eating up the fuel. I didn't count on that."

Another fifteen minutes passed. Regan found herself clenching the sides of her seat as the Cessna tossed and pitched under the increasing onslaught of the strong winds. She could feel Adam's rigid concentration as he fought to keep the plane on course. When she looked at the fuel indicator again it was alarmingly low, the arrow vibrating down.

Swallowing past the tightness in her throat, she managed a dry, shaky, "We—we're not going to make it, are we?"

This time he didn't hesitate. "No," he said truthfully, "we're all but running on fumes now. We'll have to set down. Help me to look for a clearing."

"But—"

"Just do it!"

Regan glanced over the side of the plane. The open tundra was far behind them now. There was nothing below them but dense evergreen forests. No sign of any habitation, not even a suggestion of a field. It was all wilderness and the prospect of landing in it was madness.

"Don't worry," he told her coolly. "I'm a good pilot. We'll make it."

His steely self-control in the emergency amazed her. She didn't know whether to admire his confidence or regard it as a form of insanity.

"The clearing," he reminded her.

Obediently she began searching again from her side of the craft. There were snow-clad lakes in the distance but no opening close below them that she could spot. Nothing, she thought frantically.

It was Adam who found it. "There," he said, pointing.

Her gaze followed his finger. She saw the long ribbon of a river winding through the endless forests off to the near left.

"It's our best bet," he said. "I'm going to make for that dark stretch where the winds have swept the ice clear of snow. Hang on."

He began to swing the Cessna into a landing approach, his hands hard on the yoke. The craft resisted the shift of positions, lurching angrily as the winds buffeted it now from the side.

"I don't like it, either, baby," she heard Adam mutter to the plane, "but we don't have a choice of wind direction in this."

The plane began to drift down, the forest looming toward them.

"All right," he commanded Regan, "grab my coat from the seat behind you. I want you to roll it and use it like a pillow. You get your head down on your knees, and you keep your head down until I tell you you can lift it."

"But shouldn't I watch for—"

"Damn it! Don't argue with me!"

Regan did as she was told, snatching the coat from behind her as she heard the whine of the landing gear locking down. Just before she ducked her head, her eye went one last time to the fuel gauge. The needle had hit bottom.

Adam must have seen it, too. She heard him cursing under his breath. In the next instant the engine sputtered, coughed twice, then there was nothing but a rushing silence.

Heart in her throat, Regan buried her head tightly against her knees. She could feel the nose of the plane dipping down, the jouncing and wobbling of the craft under the assaulting wind. She could sense Adam struggling to hold them steady.

Seconds later, there was the sickening thump of the wheels striking the rock-hard ice, another jolt as they skipped up and whacked down again, then the awful sensation of the plane going into a long, bumpy slide. Even muffled under his parka, she could hear the screech of the tires as he fought to apply the brakes. Regan prayed.

There was bound to be an impact. She waited for it, tensing as they coasted onward. When it came, it was less than she feared, more of a soft crumping underneath, a rough, brief rocking and then absolute stillness.

Regan didn't wait for him to tell her she could lift her head. For all she knew, he was in no condition to tell her anything. Trembling, she sat up, her eyes going immediately to the seat beside her.

He was sitting there, one arm draped negligently over the back of his seat as he faced her, looking as casual as though he had just parked the family car at a shopping mall.

"You okay?" he asked, the Texas drawl more pronounced than ever.

She nodded, feeling a bit weak, then glanced at the windows. On all sides the snow-encrusted branches of jack pines brushed against the spattered glass.

"We're in the trees," she said, bemused.

"Well, under then anyway. Our runway ended where the river makes a sharp bend here. We rolled up the bank before I could bring it to a stop."

"But you brought us safely down." She grudgingly congratulated him. "You are a good pilot at that."

He dismissed the compliment with a light, "We were lucky."

"What do we do now?" she wondered unhappily.

"We get out of here, and since we're not likely to fly out..." From a pocket in the door beside him, he extracted a folder thick with charts and maps. "Ah, this is it." He produced a detailed map of the area and spread it open across his knees.

"What are you doing?"

He didn't answer her. He was busy consulting the map. A moment later he was nodding with satisfaction. "Yep, here it is."

"Where what is?"

"Gunnerson's Fishing Camp. In the middle of nowhere like this, a map of this kind will mark any sign of civilization, even the remote fishing camps. All we have to do is follow the river eastward. It opens on a lake, and that's where this Gunnerson's Fishing Camp is located. Of course, it won't be occupied in this season, but it will give us shelter and, if we're lucky, supplies."

Regan stared at him, unable to believe what he was proposing. "You're suggesting we leave the plane and hike— No! That doesn't make sense. We've got to use the radio now. We've got to call out a distress and then stick with the plane until they come for us. And even if the radio isn't working, we're bound to be missed. They'll send search planes."

"To spot what? The Cessna is tucked under a thick canopy of trees now. I'm not about to try dragging it back out in the open, even if I wanted it to be seen from the air. Which I don't."

She went on staring at him in rising frustration. "You can't be serious! You can't mean you still intend to avoid capture! Not after this!"

"Teacher, that's just what I mean. I haven't come this far to give up now."

"But what good will it do you to hide out at some isolated fishing lodge? You can't stay there forever!"

"I don't intend to. There's bound to be boats there, canoes at least. When the ice breaks up, we'll go out on the river."

"But that could be weeks away!"

"I don't think so. I think it's just a matter of days now. It's mid-April, so it can't be long."

She shook her head over his hopeless optimism. "You're a Texan. What does a Texan know about ice breakups and the Canadian wilderness?"

The gray eyes narrowed suspiciously. "How do you know I'm a Texan?"

"I—I used to date someone from Texas. Back in college. You sound just like him. So did that police officer."

"Smart woman. Don't worry, I know enough about the north country. I was once involved in a construction project in Saskatchewan."

"That doesn't make you an expert. How do you know this fishing camp is even there? You can't be sure of just where we've come down."

"It's there," he said positively. "I had to look at the map before I took off, and I checked the landmarks all along. I had a glimpse of that lake off to the east as we came in, and a fiddle-shaped island, too, where the river widens into the lake. Just like the map."

"Be reasonable," she pleaded with him. "You can't go on running with all the odds against you."

His mouth tightened into a grim line. "I'm not running, Regan. I'm hunting."

"Hunting?" He baffled her. "What for?"

"Never mind," he told her, realizing he had probably said too much. He folded the map decisively. "All this arguing is getting us nowhere. We've got to get moving while we still have the light."

"No," she refused. "I'm not going with you. I'm staying with the plane until they find me."

The gray eyes narrowed again in displeasure. "Like hell you are. You're coming with me."

"As your hostage, I suppose."

"Yeah, that's right," he said carelessly. "I'm a desperate murderer, remember?"

Regan gulped over his reminder, but she wasn't going to let him intimidate her. "I'm staying here," she insisted.

His reaction was a surprising one this time. He chuckled. It was a sarcastic chuckle with one of those thick eyebrows elevated mockingly, but it was still a chuckle. "And just how long do you think you'd last huddled inside this plane without food or heat? In case you haven't noticed, it's already getting cold in here. After the sun goes down, the temperature will be far below freezing."

She couldn't argue with his logic. Even though she was still wearing her parka from her walk at the air station, she could feel the air turning rapidly chilly without the plane's heater.

"And give me back my coat," he added, "before I turn blue."

She thrust the rolled garment at him and watched him struggle into it as she tried to make up her mind. Maybe in her panic she was misjudging him. Maybe he was actually thinking of her well-being. On the other hand, his motive in wanting her with him could be to prevent her from telling any potential rescue party where he had gone. But, either way, did it matter? All that counted now was surviving, and perhaps his way was the best.

Oh, she hated this! She hated everything about it! But she couldn't back out of this situation as she'd backed out of Frazer Inlet. She had no choice but to deal with it somehow.

He had the parka on and was facing her again. "Well?"

"All right," she relented.

"Good." He nodded his satisfaction and then began telling her exactly what had to be done. "I'm going to drag everything out of the luggage locker. We'll go through every suitcase and every article in the plane. We sort out and take only the items we think are absolutely essential. *Nothing*," he emphasized, "that we can't easily carry in one bundle apiece. This trek is going to be tough enough without adding unnecessary baggage."

"My clothes—"

"No clothing. Not in our bundles anyway. But we'll put on as much as we can over what we're already wearing under out coats. We'll need the extra warmth."

In the next half hour, crouched in the cramped interior of the plane, they worked quickly to make two piles of objects that might be useful to them. Regan found it difficult deciding just what to take and what to leave. She was already mourning the abandonment of her precious camera. It couldn't be helped.

She tried not to think about her precarious circumstances or how much worse the situation could become before she escaped it. She tried to ignore the intimate closeness of the rugged man working beside her. Before this, there had been every reason to feel confident she would get out of this mess within a matter of hours. But now she was stranded alone with him for who knew how long. It was an unnerving realization.

She was removing items from her makeup bag when she caught him eyeing her. "Makeup?" he grumbled. "Where do you think we're headed for? A fancy ski lodge?"

Regan glared at him, holding up what she was about to add to her pile. "A supply of vitamins. A tube of lotion to prevent chapping. A small first-aid kit. Now, would you, or would you not, consider these useful?"

"I guess," he admitted without apology.

He was aggravating. How was she going to stand this ordeal with him? "And just what are you doing with my brand-new tote?"

He had emptied her roomy canvas tote bag and, with a sharp hunting knife he'd found in the bush pilot's toolbox, he was cutting slits in the sides of the bag. "Making a backpack for one of us," he answered nonchalantly.

She watched him as he hacked off a pair of the plane's seat belts, sliding the belts through the slits and knotting them inside the bag to keep them in place. He was a resourceful man anyway. That much was encouraging.

Regan produced another folded tote from inside her open suitcase and handed it to him. "Here. This one was supposed to be for all the souvenirs from Frazer Inlet that I never got around to buying. You might as well make backpacks for both of us."

At the end of the half hour, the makeshift backpacks strapped to their shoulders, they were ready to leave. Regan felt as bulky as a bear in all the layers of clothing she had added under her parka. But she was grateful for them when they left the plane and encountered the raw wind sweeping across the frozen river.

She wished she could have left a note in the Cessna telling any possible rescuers where they had gone. But Adam would have noticed her doing something like that and prevented it. In fact, she regretted all over again that they were leaving the plane at all.

They were no more than several yards away from the aircraft when she stopped and turned her head, eyeing the plane longingly where it nestled under the pines. It seemed to be the only sensible refuge there was in all this wild, forbidding landscape.

Adam, who had struck out ahead of her along the edge of the river, noticed she wasn't behind him. He turned around and came back to join her.

He stood in front of her as she faced him, his booted feet braced wide apart in a determined male stance. He was wearing a suffering expression under the knit cap hugging his dark head. "What now?" he wondered.

Regan could feel her stubbornness kicking in again. "Look, I know what you said, but I think this is a big mistake. I really do. We could be committing suicide walking away into the wilderness like this. We should stay put. Everything I've ever read about a situation like this advises you to stay put and wait."

She went on pleading eloquently, and he watched her and said nothing.

When she finally paused, he put his face down close to hers, asking a flat, "Through?"

"No, I—"

She was given no opportunity to continue her argument. Without warning, his mouth slammed over hers in a long, hard kiss that robbed her of all air. Her insides dropped like a stone.

As stunned as she was, Regan could have resisted the action. He made no effort to restrain her with his hands. Only his mouth captured her. All she had to do was step back out of his reach, drag her head away in rejection. She did neither of those things. For one mindless, impossibly reckless moment she submitted to those commanding lips locked intoxicatingly against hers, actually savored their warm breaths mingling pleasurably.

When his mouth finally released hers, Regan was too shaken to be outraged. "Wh—what did you do that for?" she asked weakly.

There was no emotion in his husky answer, as though he hadn't been affected in the least. "To change the subject. It seemed to call for something drastic. Come on, let's move."

Nothing stirred in the landscape except the wind keening through the evergreens. There was no sign of wildlife along the river, not so much as a bird calling from the trees. Regan found it a lonely place, unforgiving in its harshness. And yet it was incredibly beautiful, too, with its unbroken ranks of spruce and fir rimming the snowy riverbanks. The land was a contradiction, an enigma. Like the man trudging beside her. She didn't understand him or his abrupt shift of moods.

Whenever she showed signs of lagging as they followed the twisting river, he would urge her forward with a gruff, "Don't fall behind. We'll never get there if we don't keep moving."

Or, when she paused to adjust her slipping backpack, he would turn to her with an impatient, "What is it now?"

She wanted to slug him in those moments, tell him just what he could do with his rude demands. But she refused to give him the satisfaction of a single complaint or to let him see how scared she was, no matter how tough the going was. Nor did she raise any more objections to their arduous trek, even though she still questioned the wisdom of it. All she permitted herself to do was to silently seethe.

And then he would turn around and confuse her with an unexpected expression of genuine solicitude, asking such things as, "Are you warm enough?"

The climate was very cold certainly, but with all the layers of clothing on her and her body continually in motion, she was comfortable enough. She would nod an assurance.

Or, when the footing was particularly treacherous, either a rough stretch of ice or an unavoidable drift through which they had to wallow, he would insist on steadying her with a strong hand. As though he actually cared.

These were the worst moments for Regan. Even though the hand that helped her was gloved, she didn't trust his touch. She didn't want any repetition of that intense, bewildering emotion that had seized her when they had left the plane. She was still in a state of numbness over his startling kiss. Could still feel how she had shivered with an unwanted excitement when his hard body had leaned into hers. Could still taste his mouth so provocatively on hers.

No, she didn't understand him any more than she understood her own conflicting reactions to him. She had to keep reminding herself he was a man on the run, by his own admission an accused murderer. And yet she wasn't terrified of him anymore. He could make her furious, or he could make her pulse accelerate for a different reason, but she wasn't really afraid of him. How could that be? Could a man be a killer and still make her feel . . .

No, she didn't want to think about that!

There was one certainty anyway. For better or worse, they were in this together. Committed without choice to depending on each other for their survival. It was an awesome realization and one she didn't dare to examine too closely.

They had been on the move for better than an hour when Regan grew aware of their lengthening shadows on the snow. She stopped and looked over her shoulder, squinting against the brilliance of the sun. It was much lower in the sky now, sinking toward the vast expanse of forest. As long as they had the light and warmth of the sun they were all right, but once the sun settled over the horizon... She shuddered at the prospect of being caught out here after dark. Without shelter, they would perish in the bitter cold of nightfall.

Adam had stopped beside her, sensing her anxiety. "Your backpack slipping again?"

She shook her head. "How much farther do you suppose?"

He was evasive about it. "As the crow flies, the lake can't be all that distant. It's all these turns and switchbacks in the river. They add to the distance, but we have to stick close to the water."

She understood him. They didn't dare seek shortcuts by floundering through the thick forest where they could easily lose their way.

They pushed on along the frozen shore. They had no other choice about it. The plane was far behind them now.

Minutes later, rounding still another tight bend in the river, they saw the first evidence of civilization since leaving the plane. There, on a gravel spit reaching out from the shore, was a gray, beached vessel.

As they approached the craft, Regan could see that it was a crude version of a small houseboat. The old derelict, abandoned long ago when it had perhaps run aground on the bar, was in sad condition. Its paint had peeled away, holes were in its sides, all its equipment stripped from it and carried off.

"Come on," Adam said. "Let's look."

She was surprised that he would take even a moment of their valuable time to investigate the decaying relic. But he was already mounting the deck. She followed reluctantly.

"Careful of the planks here," he cautioned. "Some of them are pretty rotted."

Not only rotten, she thought, but in places it looked as though the porcupines had been busy chewing out meals for themselves. There was only one tiny cabin, but its door was still in place and working.

They went into the single room and found it grimy but in a fairly sound state. There were windows on either side, one with broken panes, the other still intact. A pair of wooden platforms below the windows must have once served as beds. The mattresses had vanished long ago with all the other furnishings in the bare, gloomy room.

Adam tested the floorboards of both bunks, thumping them with his fist. "Solid," he pronounced. "Not the Hilton exactly, but it will do."

He was already slinging his backpack off his shoulders as Regan watched in disbelief. "What are you doing? You're not thinking—"

"That we're going to spend the night here. Yep, that's just what I'm thinking."

"But the lake and the fishing camp—"

"Yeah, well, it's obvious we're not going to make them before dark, and we have to shelter somewhere."

She stared at him suspiciously. "You said you spotted the lake as we came down. I want to know. Just how far was it?"

"Out on the horizon."

"Out on the—That means it's way off from where we left the plane! You had me believing it was a lot closer, that we could easily make it!"

"I thought we could. I didn't count on the river twisting and turning like that."

Regan gazed around the cabin in dismay. "We're no better here than we would have been in the plane. Worse. At least the plane was tight. It didn't have a broken window with the freezing air blowing in."

"I'll fix the window."

"How? With what?"

"I can easily pry up a couple of loose deck planks out there, knock out a few rusted nails and board over the window. We'll be all right as long as we keep out the wind. With all our layers of clothing, we can last one night in here anyway."

He was being resourceful again. He was also infuriatingly nonchalant. She could have strangled him. But he was right about one thing. They couldn't move on. The light was already waning as they returned to the open deck and saw the sun beginning to slide below the trees.

"While I take care of the window," he instructed her, "you scout up some firewood. There should be plenty of dry brush close by. At least we can have a fire on the shore to warm ourselves before we bunk down for the night."

Did anyone ever tell you, Adam Fuller, that you're much too bossy?

But Regan didn't argue with him about it. She left him to deal with the window and went to hunt up the wood, grumbling under her breath as he called after her a cautionary, "And stay in sight of the boat!"

Within minutes, she had collected a pile of driftwood readily available on the gravel bar. Using dry pine needles as tinder and with matches he had given her from his backpack, she soon had a fire blazing. It felt wonderful.

Her search for wood had turned up an unexpected treasure half buried in the snow near the boat. Presumably the battered, gallon-size can had once belonged on the vessel.

Regan filled the container with snow and set it close to the fire. They would have water to drink. She had been thirsty all afternoon, and the snow she had eaten twice on their hike had not been very satisfying.

The thought of water reminded her of another urgent need. She hadn't used a bathroom since the air station, and nature was suddenly being very insistent. The only facilities offered were off in the trees.

As she left the fire and headed for the woods, she could hear Adam on the other side of the boat banging away at the window with a rock that was serving him as a hammer.

She went only far enough into the trees to fully screen herself from the boat, but the twilight was much deeper in the interior. It made her uneasy. It was equally unpleasant dealing with all her layers of clothes and feeling the frigid air on her exposed body.

She was hastily buttoning herself up when the howl of a timber wolf far off in the wilds made her stiffen with alarm. Nerves. She was a bundle of nerves. She could almost hear the voices of her family and Keith Spencer being sorry for her. "Poor Regan. Petrified, traumatized. She was never cut out to handle something like this."

The voices made her mad. She told herself with stubborn chin pointed upward that wolves weren't dangerous to people. That was only a myth. It was a small comfort.

Adam was waiting for her when she emerged from the trees, glowering his displeasure. "Where have you been? I thought I told you to stay in sight."

Here it was. Another clash of wills. She wanted to tell him he had no right to his grumpiness, that it was his fault they were out here in the middle of nowhere and she had to use the wilderness for a bathroom.

She didn't tell him that, but she didn't hesitate to baldly inform him, "I had to relieve myself."

She was surprised when his face, attractively ruddy from the cold, went even redder. He was embarrassed. Actually embarrassed by her disclosure. She almost laughed.

"Oh." He cleared his throat. "Well, come on back to the fire and supper."

"Supper?"

He produced two candy bars and a bag of peanuts from his coat pocket. "Found them in the toolbox on the plane. Our bush pilot must have had a secret sweet tooth."

The stinker! All this while he had been concealing this precious stash in his parka and had said nothing. She was famished and had been trying to forget that there would be no food until the fishing camp, and maybe not even there.

They settled side by side on a driftwood log close to the fire, eating their chocolate bars and sharing the bag of peanuts. It wasn't much of a meal, but Regan was grateful for it. She had had nothing since breakfast a lifetime ago.

The snow had melted in the can, and they shared that, too. The water had a fine sediment in it and tasted flat, but she didn't complain.

They didn't talk as they tried to warm themselves by the snapping fire in the thickening darkness. Regan finally glanced at him. His face looked brooding in the dancing glow of the firelight. He was staring into the flames, his thoughts far away.

That was why she was surprised when he suddenly said, "Your family and friends. They'll be sick with worry when the plane is reported missing, won't they?"

"Yes," she admitted. "I've been trying not to think about that."

"Is there a husband, maybe, or kids, who might be supposing the worst when you don't show up on schedule?"

"No, nothing like that. What about you?"

"I don't have a wife," he said with a strange tautness that made her sense some inner suffering. "Not anymore."

"Oh." She waited for an explanation, but he gave her none.

After another silence, he said quietly, "I'm sorry your people will have to wait and worry until you turn up for them."

He was being considerate, again. She couldn't stand this! His concern was somehow worse than his intermittent surliness. She didn't understand why this should be.

She was still trying to figure it out when they finally smothered the fire with snow, groped their way into the dark cabin on the boat and settled across their separate bunks.

Regan was exhausted from the long, grueling day and hoped that she could blot out everything, all the uncertainties, all the worries, in a heavy sleep. But sleep was impossible. Even with the broken window tightly boarded, there were icy drafts. The cabin was like a refrigerator, the cold penetrating her thick layers of clothing. Her teeth actually chattered in the darkness, and again she heard the chilling howl of the wolf far away in the forest.

She tried curling into a tight ball to benefit from her own body heat, but it was useless. No position on the hard surface helped. She was freezing. Daylight was hours away, an eternity. How was she going to last until morning?

She knew Adam was faring no better. She could hear his mutters of discomfort and the creak of his bunk across the room as he turned restlessly. And then there was a new sound. His booted feet clomping on the floor, crossing the cabin toward her.

Alerted by his movement, her head lifted, her eyes searching the blackness. She tensed, ready to challenge his nearness.

He spoke first, his voice deep and decisive. "This is crazy! We're both suffering from the cold. Move over. I'm coming in there with you."

Three

___

"**Y**ou are *what!*" Jolted by his proposal, Regan shot straight up on the bunk. She sat there shivering, both from the cold and his alarming intention.

"You heard me," he drawled. "I'm coming in there with you. And if you're popping your eyes like a weasel there in the dark, you can stop popping them. All I'm interested in is a decent night's sleep."

"Well, you're not going to get it in here with me." There was no way she was going to risk that kind of intimacy, not when she remembered how she had gone all to pieces when he had kissed her back at the plane.

"Look," he argued, "let's be reasonable about this. We could have some rough going tomorrow. We need to be rested for it, and there's no way we're going to get a wink of sleep unless we get warm. We can do that by sharing each other's body heat. Make sense?"

She had to admit that on one level it did. But on another level his plan promised an emotional disaster for her. "I don't think so," she informed him hoarsely.

"Fine. I'll go back to my bunk, and you stay in yours. When they find us here after the spring thaw, we ought to be as stiff as boards. But that's all right. At least we know they'll be saying, 'Hey, they didn't sleep together anyway.'"

Damn it! Why did he always have to be so right about everything? She hesitated, thinking about it. She was awfully cold. "Well, I—I suppose we could try it."

"Now you're being smart."

She was afraid she wasn't being smart at all, that she was about to involve herself in a situation she would very much regret.

"I don't know about this," she said nervously. "The bunk is awfully narrow. I don't see how we're both going to fit in—" Regan broke off in a fresh panic as she caught the whisper of a zipper going down in the darkness. *"What do you think you're doing?"*

"I'm taking it off," he said calmly. "I want you to take yours off, too."

"You put that zipper back up, Fuller, because—"

"Your coat," he said impatiently. "That's all I'm asking for. Your coat along with mine. What the hell did you think I was referring to?"

"I don't know. I—*Why?*" she demanded suspiciously.

She could hear him expelling his breath in exasperation. "Insulation," he explained. "I'm going to pile both coats over us to keep in our combined body heat. It's not going to work otherwise. Come on, I'm freezing here."

Regan silently complied, struggling out of her parka and thrusting it at him in the blackness. What felt like his knee nudged her in the hip. She jumped at his touch.

"Well, move over," he ordered her. "Unless you want me on top of you."

This is a mistake, she thought. I just *know* this is a mistake.

But she did as he instructed, squeezing to the inner side of the bunk until she was pressed against the cold wall. She could feel him sliding in beside her, and when his long, solid body made contact with hers it set off waves of furious flutters deep inside her vitals. The flutters intensified as his hand grazed her thigh.

He seemed to realize with that touch that she was flat on her back, her body as stiff as the board he had described.

"Not that way," he instructed. "Turn on your side with your back against my chest so we get full contact. Haven't you ever cuddled before, teacher?"

Not with an accused murderer, she wanted to tell him. But she didn't say that. What she said was an emphatic, "This isn't cuddling."

"Yeah, right, it isn't cuddling. Just turn, will you, so I can get these coats over us."

Regan did as he asked, shifting over on her right side. Hugging her arms close against her breasts, she felt him arranging the two parkas over and around them, wrapping the two of them in a snug cocoon.

The activity in her stomach became very hot when his hard length settled against her spoon-fashion. He was so tight against her that she could feel his warm breath tickling the back of her neck. Her own breath sharpened. She tried to keep very still, kept reminding herself that the male body tucked against her was fully clothed. And all she succeeded in doing was squirming unhappily.

His low growl in the vicinity of her ear didn't help. "Will you relax? Nothing is going to happen here but survival."

Damn! Adam thought. Why couldn't she stop stirring like that? All that wiggling of her warm little fanny was beginning to arouse him.

Feeling the telltale thickening in his groin, he groaned silently. With a massive restraint he willed himself not to turn hard. If she felt *that* raging against her, she'd kick him out for sure. But he was afraid he was going to lose the battle. She was killing him!

Between clenched teeth, he issued an irritable, "Stop squirming, damn you!"

Regan couldn't help it. The situation demanded a squirminess. "Sorry," she whispered. "Just trying to get comfortable. I—I'm going to settle down now, I promise."

She made a concentrated effort to keep still.

Adam was grateful. As an added measure, however, he backed the lower half of his body several inches away from hers. But, oh Lord, it wasn't easy! Not when every primal urge inside him was clamoring for him to crush himself against that soft, sweet bottom of hers.

He was going to have to watch himself with her. He was in enough of a mess as it was. He didn't need any more complications. Nor, to be fair about it, did she. So, if he could prevent it, no more situations such as tonight's. And no more mistakes such as this afternoon's outside the plane. He'd been a fool to kiss her that way. The blessing was, she hadn't noticed how powerfully the kiss had affected him. Shock waves. Shock waves that every particle of self-preservation inside him commanded him to resist. And that was exactly what he intended doing.

Beside him, Regan felt a delicious, drowsy warmth stealing over her. His makeshift sleeping bag for two was working like magic. She didn't let it bother her when the timber wolf howled again off in the distance. In her mounting languor, she even managed not to mind the disturbing body pressed against hers. All she felt as she drifted off was a pleasant sensation of security.

The muted glow of daybreak was lighting the unboarded window when Regan opened her eyes, shut them with a little gasp, and then slowly blinked them open again. She found herself staring into a sleeping masculine face less than six inches from hers, so close that she could feel his slow breath fanning her cheeks.

Sometime during the night she must have turned under the parkas, unconsciously seeking more of his warmth. But she was fully awake now, and instinct told her that she was in a highly precarious position. What she should do, she realized, was to ease herself away from his hard length without disturbing him and then immediately remove herself from this bunk.

What, in fact, she did do was to go on gazing at that slightly battered, highly appealing male face so intimately near her own. An unwise fascination, but she couldn't seem to help it. There was a dark stubble of beard on his jawline, a wonderfully stern chin and pores that were—My God, even his pores were sexy!

With a considerable effort, Regan resisted the temptation to raise one finger and trace the angles and planes of that strong face. She kept very still while she struggled to quell her baffling urges.

This was ridiculous! The man was wanted, and he had practically kidnapped her!

Evidently her careful stillness didn't matter. Without warning, she found a pair of gray eyes suddenly wide open and staring solemnly into hers. They were mesmerizing eyes. She had discovered that yesterday. She had also discovered that their shade varied with his moods. A hard silver when he was angry. A soft pewter when he was silently moody. And this morning? A smoky gray. A *smoldering* smoky gray that made her feel hot and heavy and completely self-conscious as his long, lazy gaze held hers.

"Good morning, teacher," he greeted her, his voice slow and early-morning husky. "Sleep well?"

"I—yes, fine," she mumbled, feeling a betraying flush on her cheeks.

His question jogged her memory. As a matter of fact, he had briefly disturbed her in the night, sharply calling out a name in his sleep. Not her name. Someone else's. She couldn't recall the name now, only that it had been a woman's and that he had been seeking her.

She saw a small frown gather between his eyes. "What is it?"

"Nothing." Evidently Adam had no memory of the incident, and she didn't remind him of it.

Dragging her gaze away from his compelling eyes, she stirred restlessly under the parkas. "Let me up, please. I—I need to go outside."

Her nervous haste to escape the situation amused him, but he obliged her. Rolling out of the bunk, he handed her her coat. Regan gratefully bundled into it as she left the boat and fled off into the trees.

When she returned, he was wearing his backpack and was ready to help her strap her own backpack in place.

"Aren't we going to build a fire?" she asked.

"Don't need to. It's not that cold."

He was right. The sky was overcast today, but the air was very still and definitely milder. "All the same, I'd appreciate melting some snow for water. I'd like to brush my teeth, at least."

"Brush your teeth with snow," he suggested. "I don't want us lingering here."

She could appreciate his anxiousness to move on and reach the fishing camp as soon as possible, but she didn't understand why another half hour's delay would matter. She didn't argue with him about it, though. She dug toothbrush and toothpaste out of her pack and went off to clean her teeth with snow. It was an interesting experience and one she didn't care to repeat.

When she joined him again, after hurriedly trying to work the snarls out of her hair with her pocket comb, he was waiting impatiently. He held his hand out to her.

"What is it?"

"Your share of the vitamin pills I lifted from your pack. Come on, swallow them down. It's all the breakfast we have."

Regan made a face as she accepted the vitamins. "You would remind me of how absolutely hungry I am."

"I know. I'm famished, too. But the vitamins should help."

Neither of them mentioned what they were both praying for—that they would find food of some kind at the fishing camp. Surprisingly, though, Regan decided as she struck out behind him along the frozen river, she felt physically fine. Considering all she had been subjected to in the last twenty-four hours and that she had had no proper meal since yesterday morning, she regarded this as a real achievement.

She rather regretted that self-boast several miles later as she puffed along behind him, struggling to keep up. He wasn't a whole lot taller than she was, and her legs were long for her height, but he had a stride that was like iron. She didn't see why he had to set such a punishing pace. It didn't make sense to her. She was too proud to complain about it, though. Anyway, his mood didn't invite sympathy. He had been silent and grim since leaving the boat. She didn't understand that, either.

In the end, Regan's aching leg muscles could take no more. There was a pair of flat boulders at this point along the edge of the stream. She intended to settle on one of them whether he liked it or not.

"Time-out," she called to the broad back in front of her, which was all she had seen of her companion for the past hour.

Adam stopped and turned, displaying a familiar frown. "What is it?"

"My body," she informed him obstinately. "It's sore and winded and demanding to be rested."

He considered her request. "All right, I guess we can take a short break."

"Thank you," she breathed in gratitude, sinking on the nearest boulder with a soft groan of relief.

Adam perched on an available rock, that worried frown still on his face. She gazed at him, wondering about it.

"How much farther do you suppose this lake is?" she asked him.

He shook his head. "Your guess is as good as mine. If the river would ever stop twisting, maybe we'd get there."

"What—well, what if the fishing camp isn't there?"

"It will be."

He seemed so positive about it. She tried to share his confidence. The alternative, trapped out here in the wilderness without shelter or provisions, was too frightening to consider.

But she didn't like his frown. She decided she preferred the other Adam, the one from last night and earlier this morning who had permitted her to glimpse a brief sense of humor.

Last night. It suddenly came to her then, the name he had called out in his sleep. Before she could question the wisdom of her words, Regan blurted out a rash, "Who's Jennifer?"

He stared at her, the gray eyes darkening to lead, his voice raspy with emotion. "How in hell did you—"

"You called out last night in your sleep," she said quickly.

"What did I say?" he demanded.

"Just that. Just the name."

"Oh. Well, it's nobody you need to know about."

He dismissed the subject with an emphatic briskness, but not before she noticed the shadow of suffering on his face. The same shadow she had detected last night by the fire when he had asked her about her family and friends.

"I'm sorry," she said softly. "You're right. It's none of my business."

She regretted reminding him of something that was obviously painful and perhaps connected with his fugitive state. But she couldn't help wondering about the identity of Jennifer. Was she the wife he had lost and still longed for? Or another woman who meant as much to him? And why did that idea bother her so much?

Adam got restlessly to his feet. "Come on," he urged, "it's time we pushed on again."

"But we haven't sat here more than five minutes," she objected. "What's all this urgency?"

The annoying frown was back in place on his face. "Regan," he asked her flatly, "where did you say you're from?"

"I didn't. But it's Minnesota, though I was born and raised in Winnipeg." And what did that have to do with anything? she wondered.

He nodded. "Canada and Minnesota, and you can't smell it?"

Smell? Smell what? All she could smell was the fragrance of the nearby pines, and it was a comforting aroma at that. "What are you talking about?"

"The weather."

He was crazy. "I'm urban. I don't rely on my nose for the weather. I use a TV forecaster for that."

"Well, I'm rural born and bred," he informed her dryly. "And I *can* smell an extreme change in the weather, and I've been smelling this one ever since we left the boat. We're in for a heavy precipitation all right, and at this latitude I don't think it's going to be a welcome rain off the Gulf."

"Snow? You think it's going to snow?"

"I *know* it's going to snow."

"But—" Regan swung her head, searching the landscape in disbelief. What he promised didn't seem possible. The air was still comfortable, without a breath of wind, besides which a flock of noisy chickadees was peacefully feeding off last year's seeds in a grove of white birch just behind them. None of these things was a sign of nasty weather in the making.

Adam, watching her, silently pointed upward. She lifted her head. He was right. The overcast of earlier had thickened and darkened. The sky was like heavy lead.

"Oh, Adam," she said fearfully, "it is true, if we're caught out here—" She couldn't say it. Urban dweller or not, she knew better than her companion what a Canadian blizzard in April could be like. At its worst, roaring and ferocious, life-threatening if you were stranded in it without adequate shelter.

Looking at her sherry-colored eyes widening in dismay, he regretted sharing the concern he had been withholding from her since the boat. But she had to know. She had to understand that it was imperative they keep moving, that they make every effort to reach the fishing camp as soon as possible.

Adam knew enough about Regan MacLeod by now to realize that courage wasn't easy for her, although she had been holding herself together admirably ever since he had snatched the plane. He prayed she wouldn't panic on him now as she sat there, shoulders slumped in momentary despair.

In the end she earned his approval when she straightened her shoulders and got to her feet with a decisive, "What are we waiting for?"

They pushed on along the frozen stream, silent with each other again but this time side by side. Like a team, she realized. The thought made her unaccountably glad.

She considered his forecast. Maybe he was wrong. Maybe it wouldn't snow. And even if it did snow, that didn't necessarily mean a blizzard. There was still no wind.

Less than ten minutes later, the first ominous flakes began to drift lightly through the air. Neither of them remarked on it. They trudged on as the flakes thickened into a curtain of white. The new snow began to accumulate over the crust of the last snowfall, their boots crunching through it. The stuff was wet, making the going harder. It settled in Regan's hair and on her eyelashes. She tried to adjust the hood on her parka to keep out the worst.

It helped, but only until the arrival of the wind. A bitter, searching wind. The atmosphere was suddenly no longer kind. The temperature dropped rapidly. The snow, backed by the rising wind, became a driving force, stinging, blinding. Visibility was virtually nonexistent. Only the definite banks of the river kept them on course.

Regan didn't object when his gloved hand closed around hers. She knew he intended it as a safeguard to keep them from being separated. It was merely a practical measure, but she welcomed that big hand securely clasping hers.

She stumbled against him in her growing fatigue. He caught her and held her up. And he worried. He worried about the fishing camp being there. Whatever his assurances to her, whatever the map promised, he couldn't be absolutely certain about the existence of the place, about their finding it in this hellish blizzard. And if he'd brought her out here to die... The possibility made him sick with anxiety, sick with guilt. But she didn't complain. She never complained.

How much farther? he wondered. How much longer before this damned crooked river widened into the lake?

She mumbled something. He leaned his head down to try to hear her. "What is it?"

"Dull," she said, nodding soberly. "A very dull life. That's what I had back in Minnesota. Can't complain about it being dull now, can I?"

"No," he said, smiling over her irony, "you have nothing to complain about."

Nonsense, Regan thought. There was everything to protest about. Wet snow that had worked into her boots and down her neck. Fingers and toes that were beginning to feel numb. A face that stung from a wind that howled. It was very uncomfortable. No, it was more than uncomfortable. It was downright miserable. And light-headed. She was feeling light-headed. Not a good sign. No sirree, not a good sign at all.

She made a supreme effort and roused herself, willing herself to go on. "I can do this," she said obstinately. "I can make it. I don't have to be a wimp."

"Sure you can," Adam encouraged her. "Whoever said you were a wimp?"

"People," she muttered, thinking of Keith Spencer. "Insensitive people."

"They were wrong," he assured her.

What was she talking about? he wondered. She wasn't making sense. She was weak from hunger and stress, drunk with exhaustion. He tried to support her, to keep her going. It was all he could do. That, and peer through the slashing snow for some sign of the lake where the fishing camp was located.

Regan frowned, suddenly realizing that his hand was no longer clinging to hers. Somewhere along the way he had dropped her hand in order to slide his arm around her waist. He was holding her close, bearing her sagging weight as they staggered onward.

His arm felt good around her. But it wasn't fair. It was cheating. Her valiant Scottish ancestors wouldn't like it.

"You're holding me up," she grumbled. "Why are you holding me up? I can walk by myself."

"I know," he said, his deep voice soothing her. "You've got guts."

"Damn right," she told him. "Highland grit, that's what it is."

She struggled to throw off her weary daze, to keep erect, to keep moving. He kept saying things to her. Sometimes his words were severe and demanding. Sometimes they were gentle and encouraging. Like a husband coaching his wife through a difficult labor, she decided. Nice, actually. Very nice.

She tried not to lean against him, to walk under her own power. But it was hard. The wind was so much harsher now.

"Are we going to die out here, Adam?" she asked him. "Is that what's going to happen?"

The arm around her tightened angrily. "We're not going to die," he promised her fiercely.

"But it's worse. The wind is worse."

"I know, but that's a good sign."

She laughed. He was crazy. He was crazier than she was.

"Don't you feel it?" he insisted. "We're in the open. That's why the wind is harder. It's sweeping at us over the expanse. We're on the lake now, Regan. I can't see it, but I can feel it.''

''Are—are you sure?'' she asked, afraid to be hopeful.

''I think so. I think I was even able to make out the shape of that island the map indicated when we passed it where the river widened into the lake. What we have to do now is stick to the shoreline here on our right. You can see the trees, can't you?''

''Yes,'' she said, peering at the blurred ranks of spiky, dark evergreens rising from the shore.

''We have to look for an opening in the trees, the clearing where the fishing camp is situated.''

''How far?'' she asked.

''Less than a mile I'm judging.''

God, he hoped so. He prayed he wasn't wrong, and he prayed they wouldn't miss the clearing in all this lashing snow. She was faint and dragging beside him. She couldn't last much longer. Nor, in this icy, hungry gale, could he.

In the end, it wasn't the clearing Adam spotted. It was the camp's dock hauled up on the rocky beach to protect it against the ravages of the winter ice. No sight had ever been more welcome to him.

''We're here, Regan!'' he told her triumphantly.

'''S good,'' she muttered, tiredly slurring the words. ''I hope they have beds. Not hard boards like last night. Real beds with real mattresses. *Warm* beds. You think they'll have beds, Adam?''

''Come on,'' he urged, guiding her up the beach where the trees thinned to create an opening in the forest. The snow was deeper here, making it harder to flounder through. There was a long slope. Not a steep slope, but to Regan it was like a mountain.

Adam knew she would never manage it. When she started to collapse in a drift, he caught her and swung her up into his arms. She struggled against his hold.

''No! Put me down! I have to do it on my own! The MacLeod ancestors wouldn't approve!''

What the devil was she rambling about now?

"Keep still," he ordered, managing to slap her lightly on the rump without dropping her.

She gave up the fight then and relaxed against his chest with a long sigh. Why it should feel so right to have her snuggled against him at this, of all times, was beyond him. Bearing her, he labored manfully up the slope.

"Adam?"

"What?" he grunted.

"I'm obstinate. Opinionated—and obstinate. Everyone says so. My father tells me I should stop blaming it on the MacLeod ancestors."

He grinned. He was so relieved and happy to see the dark bulk of a building taking shape through the thickly falling snow that he grinned. "You get no argument from me."

Damn! With all her layers of clothing and her backpack still in place, she was no featherweight, either. He was huffing like a blown horse when he finally crested the slope. Through tearing eyes, he could make out a porch stretched along the face of an old-fashioned log lodge.

There was one last obstacle to confront. The snow-covered steps mounting to the high porch. Adam hoisted her a little higher in his arms to secure her for the climb. It caused his beard-stubbled chin to rub against her cheek. Regan was sure it was her dreamy state that made her like the rough contact so much.

They gained the shelter of the porch, and he lowered her to the floor. She slumped against the log wall, grateful to be out of the blasting wind, and waited for him trustingly.

The windows along the front were tightly shuttered, evidence of the building's winter desertion. Adam tried the door. Locked, of course. Regrettably he would have to find someway to batter it open. And then he saw the note tacked over the door. He snatched it down and read it.

"Help yourself to the key inside the canoe," it said in a slightly legible scrawl. "Just don't let the bears read this. Yours, Ralph G."

Adam smiled. Ralph G. of Gunnerson's Fishing Camp evidently had a well-developed sense of humor. The note wasn't entirely facetious, however. Adam remembered learning in Saskatchewan, when he'd been on that construction project, that hungry bears could force their way into unlocked cabins. As for the note's casual hospitality— well, it was the code of the north country to offer shelter to anyone caught in the wilderness.

"Canoe?" he said aloud, puzzling over the key's location.

Regan, watching him, waved an arm. "Up there," she said.

He saw it then—an ancient Indian dugout canoe suspended by heavy chains from the rafters of the porch's ceiling. He stood beneath the canoe, drew his glove away with his teeth, and stretched his hand up inside the craft, searching along its length through bits of dried leaves that had blown there last fall. His fingers closed at last around the key.

He hurried to insert it into the lock. They both needed to get inside, find a way to get warm. The door opened without effort. He threw an arm around Regan and helped her into the dark interior of the lodge.

There was nothing to be seen in the thick gloom until he raised a pair of sash windows and folded back the shutters. They found themselves in a spacious lounge. The place felt colder than the outside. But the one thing that mattered was prominently there—a cavernous stone fireplace whose hearth was heaped with firewood.

"I—I've never been so glad to see anything in m-my life," Regan said, standing as close to the fireplace as she could get, as if its hearth was already blazing with blessed heat.

Adam glanced at her. She was shivering like a hypothermia victim. He had to get her warm. He had to get both of them warm.

There were fireplace matches in a can on the mantel and kindling in a wood box. He crouched down on the hearth and quickly laid a fire in the grate. Within seconds, flames were licking at the pyramid of birch logs. Setting the screen in place, he got to his feet.

Regan hadn't moved. Glassy-eyed, she stared at the leaping flames, her nose wrinkling with pleasure at the aroma of the curling wood smoke. She was still shivering.

There was a colorful Indian blanket thrown over the back of a sofa. Adam snatched it up and spread it on the floor in front of the fire.

"Come on," he ordered. "Down on the blanket."

In silent obedience she sank to the floor and huddled there on the blanket, her gaze never leaving the fire. Casting off his backpack and parka, he knelt in front of her. He helped her out of her own pack, then stripped off her gloves and boots. She came to life when he began to peel away her double layer of wet socks.

She started to pull back, objecting through teeth that still chattered, "I—I can do this myself. I don't need help. Damn it, I can do anything!"

"That's right," he said. "But just now *anything* means keeping still. Your feet are like ice. Think I want you getting sick on me? You're enough of a pain as it is, teacher."

He was taking charge, Regan realized. Helping her again in that gruff way. What was she going to do about him?

His big hands began briskly rubbing her feet, holding them firmly against his hard thighs. It felt good, she decided. It felt awfully good. She sighed in pure animal enjoyment.

A sweet warmth began to seep through her. She could feel life in her limbs again, feel her head clearing. The fire and Adam's attention were restoring her sanity. She was going to be all right.

He went on working on her feet, a gentle, relaxing massage now. She looked at his dark head bent over his task, and something swelled inside her. Something that was both frightening and exhilarating at the same time. And then it struck her with a forceful clarity—the truth about Adam Fuller!

Four

This man hadn't killed anyone! He was no more capable of murder than she was. He might be accused of the crime, but he hadn't done it. She was convinced of that.

Why? Regan wondered. Why was she so certain of his innocence? Because he could be as caring as this? Because she sensed that under all the abruptness was an intrinsically decent man who respected life?

Could she trust her judgment? Or was she being deceived by a pair of strong hands deeply stroking her flesh? By her toes digging tantalizingly into his rock-hard thighs?

She went very still, hardly daring to breathe as she realized that what was happening was no longer just a restorative process. The slow heat of his thighs and the lazy sensuality of his caressing fingers awakened a glow deep inside her. And she didn't know what to do about this mellow, aching sensation.

This was a risky business, Adam decided. At one point, when he had leaned over her, he had caught the faint fragrance of her silky, russet hair. Now, fondling her this way, because he knew suddenly that was exactly what he was doing, made his gut tighten with a restless longing. Hell of a moment to feel desire. All wrong.

His hands stopped moving on the smooth, soft skin of her arches. But he didn't withdraw his fingers. He allowed them to linger there against her seductive warmth, teasing himself with the temptation of the moment.

Mistake, they both thought. And, simultaneously, as though they had been stung in the same instant, they jerked back from each other.

"You feeling any warmer now?" he asked, his voice quick and rough.

Her own words, equally self-conscious, tumbled concurrently over his. "I'm feeling warmer now."

There was a long pause while they avoided each other's gazes and struggled for a safe communication.

It was Adam who saved the moment with a careful, offhand, "Are you recovered enough to face the question of whether we eat?"

She welcomed his suggestion with an eager, "Yes, please. My stomach is as hollow as a drum."

"Then let's investigate."

Regan had no choice but to slip back into her damp boots. "Which way?" she wondered, coming to her feet beside him.

"Let's try back here."

He led the way past a dining area with a large oak table that could easily accommodate a dozen people. She followed him through a swinging door into another darkened room.

"Let there be food, oh, let there be food," she prayed aloud while Adam opened the shutters to give them light.

They found themselves in a kitchen that looked like something out of a museum. There was a ponderous black wood stove intended for heating rather than cooking. The cooking was apparently done on a kerosene range against the opposite wall. In the absence of electricity, an assortment of oil lamps was lined up on a counter. There was a sink, too, with a hand pump mounted at its side. Hopefully, Adam thought, it would offer them a water supply. Providing, that is, he could figure out how to prime it.

Regan began flinging open cupboard doors. There were dishes and utensils of every description, but nowhere was there a sign of food. Not, anyway, until she investigated the area behind another door.

"Adam," she called excitedly, "bring a lamp! I think we've struck pay dirt!"

He joined her after lighting one of the lamps. "What have you got?"

"It's a pantry! And it looks like a well-stocked pantry, too! Oh, my, look at that!"

"What?"

"All these old tins on the shelves. My mother collects old tin advertising. She'd go wild in here."

"The heck with that. I want to know what's inside them."

They began prying the lids off the cans lining the open shelves on both sides. There were several kinds of pastas, beans, rice, cornmeal, oatmeal, salt, sugar, flour, tea, powdered egg, powdered milk, a variety of crackers, even nuts and dried fruits. Enough provisions to last them for days.

"Is there coffee?" Adam asked. "Do you see coffee anywhere?" I'd kill for a cup of coffee."

"I don't—Oh, wait, here it is! We're in luck! Bless old Ralph G. Adam, there's everything here that could safely go through the winter without freezing or spoiling. Why would they leave so many provisions?"

"It's the code of the north working again. Shelter and food for anyone who might wander in out of a blizzard."

"Well, that's us all right. Adam, could we eat? I'm starving."

"As soon as I get that pump and range working. How are your cooking skills? Mine are pitiful."

"Not good enough to teach home economics, but you won't know the difference when I dish you up a plate of beans and rice."

He didn't either when they later settled in front of the fire with their heaping plates of red beans and seasoned white rice. The kitchen was still much too cold for comfort, so they chose to eat in the lounge, sitting cross-legged on the floor close to the blazing hearth, their plates balanced across their knees.

Adam, tucking into the fare she had prepared, took time between mouthfuls to utter a pleasurable, "Ah, better than grits and gravy."

Regan smiled. Grits and gravy, huh? Well, he had indicated he'd been born and bred in rural Texas. Having never tasted that particular Southern dish herself, she had no comparison. But right now anything would taste good, even simple beans and rice. She ate her meal with a relish that matched his.

Funny, she thought, how the basic comforts you took for granted at home could seem so miraculous in a place like this. Food, shelter, warmth. The lodge, though rudimentary in its equipment, offered them all of these essentials.

And the unexpected as well, she soon realized. Having savored the last bite on her plate, she took the opportunity to gaze at her surroundings. She was amazed at what the rustic lounge contained. Stuffed into every corner and across every surface were Indian artifacts of every description. Baskets, beaded moccasins, pottery, feathered masks, even a pair of antique snowshoes high on the log wall under the enormous head of a stuffed moose that seemed to stare down at her balefully.

"My word," she said, fascinated, "do you suppose there are totem poles in the bedrooms upstairs?"

Adam's rich, robust laughter both startled and gladdened her. Until now, the only amusement he had demonstrated had been of the dry, cynical variety. But this was an honest, open humor, an indication that perhaps there was more than just frost around his heart.

"Remembering the Indian dugout on the porch," he drawled easily, "I wouldn't be surprised."

She laughed with him. "I'm getting the distinct impression that our Ralph Gunnerson is something of a character. Oh, look under the window! An old-time windup phonograph! Do you suppose it works?"

He didn't answer her, and she glanced at him. He had emptied his plate and set it aside. He was now stretched full-length on his side across the Indian blanket, his head propped up with one hand. Ignoring his mug of coffee, he watched her. All traces of amusement had vanished.

Regan, meeting his sober gaze, swallowed past the disturbing tightness in her throat. There was a speculation in those potent gray eyes that reminded her of the threatening moment earlier when he had warmed her with his hands.

The snugness the fishing lodge offered them no longer seemed safe and restful to her. No longer a place of simple, cozy refuge. She remembered she was here alone with him, that they could be like this for days. Just the two of them cut off from the world. And the thought of their isolated togetherness, all that it could potentially involve, panicked her. Maybe she was being a coward again, but she couldn't help it. Facing physical danger was one thing, but confronting something like *this* . . . Well, she wasn't made for a provocative situation, didn't know how to handle it. She had the sudden urge to escape.

Dragging her eyes away from that lean male form lounging there with such lazy, virile appeal, she got quickly to her feet. She began to move around the room, investigating cabinets, poking behind cupboard doors.

Adam, watching her, sensed a frantic quality in her search. After a moment he realized what she was hunting for. What he failed to understand was her true reason for needing to locate it.

"You won't find it, Regan," he told her quietly.

She turned around, looking innocent but avoiding the directness of his gaze. "I was just exploring."

He swung back into a sitting position, his voice hard with disappointment in her. "Like hell. You were looking for a two-way radio, weren't you? I imagine they keep one here in season. They'd have to have some way of communicating with the outside. I also imagine, rather than risk damage to it from the winter cold and damp, they take it with them when they leave in the fall. Looks like you're stuck, after all. No way to call out for help."

She didn't answer him. She was too busy being surprised at his talent for reading her so accurately. She didn't know that Adam completely misunderstood her sudden longing to get away from the lodge.

Fine, he thought bitterly. So she still didn't trust him. All she could think about was putting distance between herself and a hunted man. Well, he didn't need her trusting him. After what he had experienced back in Texas, he considered that sort of man-woman relationship just so much garbage anyway.

Whether he admitted it or not, though, her behavior felt like a rejection to him. It roused a sudden loneliness in him. He found himself thinking of Jennifer. He missed her, worried about her. He wondered when he would see her again.

Regan, hovering by one of the windows, was distressed by the expression on his face. The shadow of suffering was back in his eyes. She couldn't bear his pain. She forgot about the radio. All she wanted now was to ease his unhappiness, turn his mind away from the dark thoughts that were haunting him again. The weather was a convenient distraction.

"Adam," she informed him softly, "it's stopped snowing."

His gaze went to the widow beside her. He nodded slowly. "So it has. In that case . . ." He got to his feet, reaching for his coat on the sofa.

She was relieved to see him shake away his black mood. "Where are you going?"

"Outside. I think I glimpsed some other buildings behind the lodge when we arrived. I ought to check them out, see what they have to offer before it gets dark. With any luck there will be a wood supply somewhere. What we have here won't last more than another day."

"Can—can I come with you?"

He hesitated, then decided that it didn't matter. "If you don't mind going back out to tramp through snow."

He knew he was ready to forgive her about the radio. Why should he blame her for wanting to get out of this mess, for being anxious to get away from a man who was an accused murderer?

He was accepting her company, Regan realized as she struggled into her gear. But he was stiff about it, and returned to being the stranger. That bothered her, and she didn't understand why she should care so much.

They went through the kitchen, leaving the lodge by way of an enclosed service porch. They stood for a moment in the clearing outside as they viewed their surroundings, their breaths smoking in the atmosphere. The wind had dropped, but the temperature was even lower than before. Regan could smell the cold, pure and still and crisp. Every twig was laden with the newly fallen snow. A true winter wonderland. Except this was April.

There was a collection of various structures nestled under the tall pines. The nearest was an open-sided shed bulging with firewood.

"We're in luck again," Adam observed, gratefully eyeing the wood.

Regan followed him as he led the way past the shed toward a pair of small log cabins facing the lake. He had found a ring of keys hanging in the kitchen. One of the keys unlocked both cabins. They proved to be bunkhouses for guests who came to the fishing camp in the summer.

Moving on, they reached a small storage building. This turned out to be more interesting. Ralph Gunnerson was a true collector. The place was stuffed with junk of every variety. Some of it useful, Adam noted. Fishing gear, of course, and lots of tools. Somewhere in all this mess he hoped to locate a shovel. He would need to clear a few paths for them tomorrow.

"I guess this doesn't surprise me," Regan said, picking up a bow and a quiver of arrows.

Adam grunted over the sight of the bow and arrows. "Not my style. Now, if it were a rifle I might try hunting some game for us."

"Would there be guns somewhere in the lodge?" she asked, not liking the idea.

He shook his head. "Not likely. They would have wisely removed any firearms along with their radio."

He was giving her the entrée she had been looking for since leaving the plane. "What about the revolver you took off that policeman?"

He smiled at her dryly. "You can stop worrying, Regan. I left it back at the air station. I'm in enough trouble as it is. I didn't want them thinking I'm armed and dangerous, some desperado to be shot down on sight."

"Oh," she said, casually replacing the bow and quiver. But she was relieved. More than that, she had a renewed respect for him.

"You ready to move on?" he asked.

"Yes. No, wait. Look there. It's a tin hip bath, isn't it? Old as the hills, I bet. You don't suppose that's the one and only facility on the premises?"

"Showers," he said.

"You're kidding!"

"I am not. Come on, I'll show you."

He led the way toward another structure situated near the log cabins. "A common bathhouse," he said, indicating a pressure tank raised on stilts. "Probably in the summer they pipe the water up straight out of the lake. It would only need a small gas generator.''

''Beats a tin tub, I guess, but it's still pretty primitive.''

''The people who fly up here and land on that lake aren't looking for home comforts, Regan. In fact, this is just the scene they want, roughing it in the trackless wilderness for a few days far from civilization.''

She sighed. ''Sounds depressingly familiar. My family used to have a cabin on the lake back in Minnesota. Everybody loved it. Except me. I always went there under protest. Wood stoves, an outside privy just like that one over there, no modern plumbing. I'm afraid I didn't cope with any of it very well.''

''You're coping with it here,'' he pointed out.

She didn't answer him. He looked at her, watching her as she slowly chewed on her lower lip. He understood something about her then. Regan MacLeod was deeply insecure about herself. He wondered why he should suddenly feel such empathy for her.

The lounge windows framed the hard, bright light of a clear morning when Regan stirred and opened her eyes. For a moment she lay there under the double layer of blankets, stretching muscles that were stiff after yesterday's long ordeal. Otherwise, she felt completely recovered.

Adam had dragged down a pair of mattresses from the bedrooms upstairs. They had spent the night on the floor in front of the fireplace where they could keep warm. She turned her head to check on her companion. He was still deep in sleep on the neighboring mattress, one arm flung over his head as he faced her on his side.

She had learned yesterday morning on the derelict boat that it was a mistake to watch him in this attitude. It did things to her insides that left her in a helpless turmoil.

But they weren't sharing each other's body heat this morning. A good three feet separated their mattresses. She didn't think it could hurt to spend a brief moment considering him. She was wrong.

Under the dark, tousled hair was a face softened in sleep, the hard lines of grief and care wiped away, making him look younger and more vulnerable. And also blatantly, frustratingly sexy.

Regan squirmed under the blankets, struggling to oppose the tender longing swelling inside her. How was she supposed to withstand the tension of sleeping nightly so close to him? It was a necessity if they were to keep warm, but it was pure torment. She acknowledged her desire for him now. She also knew that any involvement was out of the question. Guilty or not, he was still a man on the run, and she had no business getting close to him. Besides, there was someone called Jennifer.

Willing herself to resist the situation, she slipped quietly off the mattress and went to tend the fire. There were still hot coals in the grate. She added fresh logs and replaced the screen.

She was careful not to disturb Adam. She knew that he had gotten up periodically through the night, sacrificing his rest in order to keep the fire going for them. He deserved to sleep now without interruption.

Hugging the blanket around her to ward off the chill air, Regan padded softly to the window and looked out. The sun off the snowy plain of the lake was blindingly brilliant, the sky a brittle blue. The beauty of the white landscape, etched by the masses of dark evergreens, was breathtaking. And almost painfully peaceful.

Reluctantly she turned from the view and headed toward the kitchen with breakfast on her mind. The kitchen was shockingly cold, but she knew from her days at the family cabin how to manage the wood stove. And Adam had showed her how to work the kerosene range and the sink's water pump.

She got a good fire going in the stove and was starting toward the pantry when she changed her mind. Breakfast could wait. There was something else in this moment that she wanted more. No, make that *needed* more.

She hesitated, glancing through a back window toward the storage building at the edge of the clearing. She remembered what she had confided out there yesterday to Adam. In effect, she had admitted her lifelong inability to cope with anything alien or intimidating. That feeling of inadequacy suddenly made her very angry.

Damn it, it was time she overcame that old problem. She could make a start in that direction right now by handling this next little job on her own. How difficult could it be? Her ancestors had probably managed it daily.

With determination, Regan slipped back into the lounge to fetch her coat and boots.

Adam roused himself, blinking at the glare of morning light slanting through the uncurtained windows. Sitting up on his makeshift bed, he glanced toward the other mattress. Regan wasn't there. He wondered if she was in the kitchen. He lifted his head, sniffing around in hope of catching the aroma of breakfast cooking. He was ravenous. He also badly needed a shave. The two-day-old growth of beard on his face was beginning to itch.

The only thing he could smell was wood smoke. The fire had been freshly fueled. Pulling himself together, he left his bed and started toward the kitchen in search of Regan.

He came through the swing door and stopped in surprise. The wood stove was glowing with warmth, and on the kerosene range was an enormous kettle of bubbling water putting wisps of steam into the air. More puzzling was the trail of melting snow. It led from the back door, across the kitchen floor and under a blanket that was pinned on half the length of a clothesline stretched across one end of the room. From behind this curtain came the sounds of splashing.

She must have heard the hiss of the swing door. She called out to him over the screening blanket, "Stay on your side, please."

"What are you doing back there?" he demanded, venturing a little farther into the room.

"What do you think? Taking a bath, of course." There was no reaction from him. Nothing but dead silence from his side. "You're surprised, aren't you?"

"Yeah, I—I'm surprised all right," he stammered in a voice that nearly strangled him.

She couldn't know *how* surprised, Adam thought. His new position in the room had suddenly provided him with a view she was entirely unaware of. There was a window down at the exposed end of her contrived bathroom. Its outside shutter was still closed, making a good mirror out of the glass. From his angle in the room, Adam was able to discern her reflection. It left nothing to the imagination. He could feel the slow heat rising in him as he stood there, rooted to the floorboards.

"You sound funny," she said. "Anything wrong?"

"No. Just—just early-morning hoarseness, I guess."

"Oh. Well, anyway," she went on innocently, telling him all about it, "it surprised me, too. After two days without proper washing I couldn't stand myself, and I knew there was no chance in this season of getting those showers out there working for us. So I just decided to do something about it. I hauled that tin bathtub out of the storage shed, across the clearing and right up here into the kitchen. You should have seen me dragging it." She chuckled in recollection. "It wasn't so heavy, but it was awfully awkward. I kept landing on my backside in the ice and snow. I'll probably pay for it with a sore bottom."

Her bottom looked just fine to him. Better than fine. She was standing now in the tub to rinse herself off, her back to the betraying window. He could see the creamy, satiny fullness of her naked hips, the sleekness of her calves and thighs. His hunger for food was forgotten as another, more demanding appetite gripped him.

"It was pretty funny," she said. "In all that bulky stuff I was wearing I had a heck of a time rolling around and trying to rock myself back on my feet. Now I know what a pregnant woman must go through." She laughed again. "Anyhow, I managed it all, including heating up enough water for a decent bath. I know it's just a small achievement, but I'm still kind of proud of myself."

She turned in the tub, reaching for a dipper on a stool. The lush mounds of her breasts came into his view, their peaks rose-tipped, enticing. Droplets of water clung to the smooth swell of her firm belly, trickling down in little rivulets to the intriguing, shadowy mystery at the juncture of her thighs. He felt the lust surging through him in thick, powerful waves.

"Hey," she wondered after another silence, "you still there?"

"Yeah," he said thickly, "still here."

He shouldn't be. He knew he shouldn't be. He was a bastard for standing there in that fashion, gaping at her as if he were some excited adolescent peeping through a forbidden crack, all hot and bothered by the sight of female flesh in the raw. But *her* flesh . . . well, she was magnificent with those long legs and that rich hair tumbling around her bare shoulders.

"Oh," she remembered, "something interesting. When I went looking for towels upstairs, I found some clothes left behind in the bedroom closets. Maybe we can make use of them. Slippers and a couple of robes anyway. Sweatshirts, too. Shouldn't matter about size with those."

"Uh, right," he agreed.

He should back away before she looked up and toward the window and caught his own reflection staring at her. He should back away right now. He didn't. He went on feasting his eyes on her. She was using the dipper, scooping up water to pour over her soap-slick skin. The sight drove him wild.

"I'm just about finished here," she reported. "I'm going to leave my hair for the sink later on. I put more water on the range, though. I figured you'd want a bath of your own."

"That—that's fine."

Oh, God, she was stretching! Arching her body in languorous pleasure like a kitten after its bath. Her milky breasts lifted with the movement, the nipples thrusting high. Adam felt himself go painfully hard.

"Do you know," she was saying, "we could probably do it right here on the kitchen table."

"*What?*" he choked.

"Aren't you listening? I said we could set up breakfast in here, now that the kitchen is warm."

She didn't miss his low groan of anguish.

"What's the matter?" she asked, reaching for a bath sheet. "Hungry, I bet. Well, look, I'll fix breakfast while you have your bath. With the water already hot it shouldn't take long. I figured oatmeal. What do you think?" There was no answer. "Adam?"

The swish of the swing door announced his hasty exit from the room. Regan, toweling herself dry, slipped into a scratchy woolen robe several sizes too big for her and came around the blanket. The kitchen was empty all right. Now what on earth had made him race off that way without a word? Was he mad about something? It was difficult to tell. The man had more mood swings than a touchy bear.

She went behind the curtain again, regretting the necessity of getting back into her same clothes. There was no choice about it, though.

She was dressed and wondering how she was going to manage to empty the tub when she heard a whacking noise out back. She went to the nearest unshuttered window and looked out.

Adam was across the yard at the woodshed. He'd found an ax and a block, and he was splitting logs in a kind of grim frenzy. She watched for a moment in bewilderment as he swung the tool in powerful downward strokes, driving it into the upended logs as if he were a man striving to release an awful frustration. Again and again the ax lifted and plunged.

He's crazy, she thought. Why would he be making more firewood when there's already a mountain of firewood out there?

She gave up trying to figure that one out and turned away from the window. Since he was more interested at the moment in firewood than a bath, she decided to leave the emptying of the tub until after breakfast. She needed to light another burner on the range to cook the oatmeal, but she had used the last of the kitchen matches when she'd fired the wood stove. There were plenty of matches in the lounge, though.

Regan was at the front of the lodge, reaching for the can of long matches on the fireplace mantel, when she was arrested by a sound from outside. Not the ax cracking against wood. This was a different noise. Heart beating fast with sudden hope, she rushed to the porch door and flung it wide. She stood there in the doorway, listening, straining to identify what she was hearing in the near distance overhead.

It was louder now, clearer and unmistakable. The drone of an approaching light aircraft! A rescue plane searching for them! It had to be!

She didn't think. She only acted. Spurred on by the chance of being reunited with her family, who must be supposing every horror about her, she snatched up her parka from the stair railing where she had earlier draped it. She struggled into it and flew across the porch and down the steps.

The trees hid the lodge. She had to get down the slope and out on the open lake where the plane could see her. She was already yelling and waving her arms as she ran. She didn't hear the pounding of boots from behind her, didn't pay any attention to the angry shouts at her back.

Regan had played football as a kid with her brothers, but it had always been the touch variety. She didn't know what it was like to be tackled. When that strong force behind her punched into her legs, dragging her to the ground, it was such a shock that she went down with a loud, "Woof!"

She wasn't hurt, wasn't even knocked breathless by the impact. The fluffy snow in which the two of them landed under the pines prevented that. But she was outraged. Outraged and determined.

"*Nooo!*" she howled, managing to twist over on her back under the arms locked around her legs. "Let me up! Don't you understand? It's a plane! They must be looking for us!"

"You're not going to signal them!" Adam told her savagely, crawling up over her length as he struggled with his full weight now to subdue her heaving body. "I told you I wasn't going to be taken again! I meant it!"

In a fierce panic now, because she could hear the plane's engine directly overhead, she squirmed and kicked against his restraint. "I won't let you stop me!" she wailed. "This could be our chance! Our *only* chance of getting out of here alive!"

"Regan, stop fighting!" he commanded, swearing at her violently as she tried to bite his wrist. "I told you we'll get out of here, and we will!"

"I don't believe you! Oh, God," she pleaded frantically, 'You've *got* to let me up!"

"It's too late," he informed her, relaxing his grip on her. "Hear? They're going away."

He was right. The sound of the engine was already dwindling. She could have wept with frustration and disappointment. She sagged down into the snow, glaring at him accusingly. "We've missed it. We've missed the whole opportunity, and we might never get another one."

"We'll get out," he promised her. "As soon as the lake and river open up, we'll get out."

"How?" she demanded sullenly. "You said there would be boats here, and there aren't any. We haven't seen a single boat except that rotting dugout on the porch."

"There are boats," he insisted, nodding in the direction of the lake. "There's a boat house built into the shore just below that stand of spruce. I had a glimpse of it yesterday from an upstairs window. This is a fishing camp. There have to be boats."

She didn't say anything. She went on looking at him, wanting to believe him and not certain she could. He was levered above her, resting his upper weight on his elbows on either side of her. It was safe now to let her up. But he didn't move, and she didn't ask him to. His legs were still tangled with hers. She was suddenly aware of his groin intimately squeezed against hers. She liked the sensation, liked it a lot, but it worried her.

Adam gazed at her. There were tears welling at the corners of her eyes. The sight of them stirred something in him that was both protective and possessive, a warm, liquid male yearning at the pit of his stomach.

"I know you're scared," he told her, his voice soft and husky. "But I promise you, Regan, I won't let anything happen to you. We will survive, and we will get out."

"I know," she whispered. "I—I trust you."

Oh, Lord, he thought. She shouldn't. She shouldn't trust him at all, because he suddenly, desperately wanted to—

Reason vanished. Self-control vanished. With a low moan, his body sank over hers until he was fully covering her length. He felt her struggling beneath him, and it was a moment before he understood her battle. Not resistance. Not this time. She was only fighting to release her pinned arms. And then those arms were free and clasped around him, pulling him tightly down to her, holding him close.

It was all the encouragement he needed. His mouth settled urgently against hers, stilling her little gasp as he took her in a deep, searing kiss.

With the barriers between them eradicated, they both went wild with passion. Adam's hands were all over her, driving through her thick hair, stroking eagerly down her sides and hips, digging under her coat in a futile effort to get next to that flesh that had inflamed him in the kitchen. He couldn't achieve what he wanted, not nearly, not out here in the snow. But he had her mouth, and he made the best of that.

He went on kissing her without interruption, his tongue meeting hers with quick, wanton thrusts. She tasted sweet and warm and moist, and he groaned with the need to bury himself in her. Groaned because she was clinging to him, writhing under him, her legs wound around him.

Regan, holding him shamelessly in her total grip, had never been kissed with such consuming abandon, had never been so intensely aroused by a man before. She was past shock, past caring about anything but the marvelous feel of him. The glory of his mouth against hers, the roughness of his beard, the rocky bulge of his desire strained against her longingly. It was all crazy and reckless and wonderful.

She was never certain at what instant it went wrong. She just knew that his hands were suddenly no longer there at the sides of her face, holding her head steady as his mouth worked a wet magic on hers. He had stopped kissing her. His body was not heating hers. There was nothing between them but frigid air. Regan was conscious of a profound loss.

Her vision clearing with a return to sanity, she gazed up at him in confusion. His body had tensed and reared back. He was staring down at her, and there was a tightness in his expression. There was also a seething emotion in his eyes. It took her a moment to realize that it was anger, and that the anger was directed at her.

Five

Regan suddenly understood his resentment. He was blaming her for the raw, uninhibited passion that had momentarily cost him his self-control. *Unfairly* blaming her.

What she didn't understand was why he blamed her at all, why he had pulled back from her when his desire for her had been so evident, when he must have realized she had wanted him with the same compelling need. She felt hurt and rejected. And not very brave about what was happening to her. Not any of it. Not this or all that had preceded it since she had boarded that plane in Frazer Inlet.

Swallowing the infuriating lump in her throat that threatened to bring tears, which she refused this time to shed, she managed to croak a low, "What's wrong? What have I done?"

"Nothing," he said curtly. "You haven't done a thing."

He drew away from her and got to his feet, leaning over to extend a helping hand. She ignored his offer and got up from the snow on her own, dusting herself off. She didn't believe him, not when he was so stiff and remote from her.

"Then why are you angry?" she challenged him.

"Regan, I'm angry with me, not you."

It was true, he realized. He was responsible for initiating that momentary insanity, not her. And if for a few seconds there he had actually blamed her for being an irresistible temptation...well, that was hardly her fault. He was the fool for forgetting his circumstances, for not remembering he was a man who was accused, hunted. No woman deserved to be involved with something like that.

Thank providence that a warning had sounded inside his head when it had, that he had exercised a massive restraint just in time. God, he had been about to take her right out here in the open, regardless of snow or cold.

He wasn't going to forget again. He was going to do whatever it took to avoid any further intimacies. He couldn't risk another scene similar to this one. Not with her. He didn't want to hurt her. Maybe he was beginning to care about her. Care a lot. And that, too, was a mistake.

"I'm sorry," he muttered. "It won't happen again."

He swung away from her and headed for the lodge. Regan, watching him stride off, spent a long moment being unhappy and bewildered. Then, disgusted with her old cowardice, she made up her mind. She wasn't going to let him get away with this. She wanted some answers. She *deserved* some answers.

She found him, with coat shed, and down on his haunches, repairing the fire when she marched into the lounge and confronted him.

"Adam," she demanded, "I think I'm entitled to an explanation. Not just about what happened out there but about...well, everything. I didn't ask to be in this situation we're in. But since I am in it, and with no way out of it, then I feel I have the right to know, to understand it."

He replaced the screen in front of the fire, got to his feet and slowly faced her, his hands thrust into the pockets of his cords. The expression on his face was rigid, obdurate. "You know all you need to know about me . . . that I'm a wanted man accused of murder."

"I know more than that."

"What? What else do you think you know?"

"That you're not a killer. That you *couldn't* be a killer."

The hands jammed into his pockets balled into tight fists. He smiled at her grimly. "Not very smart, teacher. If I were you, I'd go on believing the worst about me."

Why couldn't she understand? he asked himself. Why couldn't she see that it wasn't safe for her to be any more involved with him than absolutely necessary? If she knew the truth, understood any of the details, she could be charged as an accessory in aiding his escape.

"You're not going to tell me, are you?" she asked.

If she refused to be reasonable about it, then he was just going to have to be sensible for her. "That's right," he drawled. "I'm not going to tell you."

"What are you doing?" she wanted to know.

He was dragging his mattress away from the fireplace, heading with it toward the kitchen. "I'm putting this in the kitchen. I'll sleep in there from now on."

"But that means keeping both fires going all night."

"Maybe, but it's also a lot less risky." He paused to regard her. The smile on his face was cynical, almost nasty. "A man and a woman stranded alone like this . . . Well, it's a pretty alluring setup, isn't it? Especially when there's an element of danger about it. Not that I'm against engaging in a bit of old-fashioned lust when it comes my way. Because what almost happened out there was exactly that, and no more. But in my present situation, sweetheart, I can't afford to be occupied with anything but staying out of jail."

Regan was looking at him as though he had slapped her across the face. He had been deliberately cruel, and he hated himself for that. But it was better if she was momentarily hurt by the half-truth he had just stung her with than to be permanently hurt by an affair that could go nowhere.

* * *

They spent three awful days being carefully polite to each other. They also kept out of each other's way as much as possible. Adam stayed outdoors much of the time, shoveling a network of paths they didn't need and making endless firewood. Regan remained indoors where she played solitaire in front of the fireplace, tried to read the only book in the place, which was a lengthy, boring fishing guide, and quietly went out of her mind.

When, by necessity, they did come together for mealtimes, or to briefly discuss essentials, the tension between them was like the charged atmosphere before a storm.

Regan had figured out by now that the humiliation he had inflicted on her that morning had been largely for her own benefit, not his. The exasperating man was protecting her again, just as he had been trying to take care of her since they had landed in this mess, even at the expense of his own image. Damn it, how could she ever be less than a wimp when everyone insisted on treating her as though she were something fragile?

Her realization about Adam's motives should have softened the tension. Instead, it made her more restless. He was right, of course. In his circumstances, it would be a mistake to surrender to their desires. But his nearness was driving her crazy. She wanted to get away from the effect he was having on her treacherous senses. She wanted to be out of this painful dilemma, not trapped here with a rugged man whose every word and look were making her desperate. The waiting with him was pure torture.

There was no sign of another rescue plane, if in fact, the plane that morning had been searching for them. A low and persistent overcast since then might have been responsible for that. Or perhaps searchers were looking farther east along the route the Cessna was supposed to have been flying.

In any case, Adam didn't want rescue. He was counting on a breakup of the ice. It was true that each day seemed milder than the last and that they'd had no fresh snowfall, but there was no sign on the lake of the ice breakup.

It was on one of those mild days, their fourth at the camp, that Regan decided she could no longer avoid an unpleasant chore that had been demanding attention almost since their arrival. They needed clean clothes. Both of them had managed to cram an extra set of underwear each in their backpacks before leaving the plane, and they'd worn the layers of outer garments, which gave them a couple of changes. But all of these things by now, including the few articles they'd found in the upstairs bedrooms, needed washing.

The laundry facilities were as quaint and antiquated as everything else in the lodge: a washing board and a tub hanging on the service porch. Adam offered to help with the job, but he was already doing all of the heavy work, including the nightly washing of their dishes. She bravely declined his offer and then regretted her generosity when she found herself bent over the kitchen sink, soaking and scrubbing their load of garments in primitive pioneer-fashion.

Actually the hard part was Adam's briefs. She hated to admit what handling his intimate garments did to her libido, but the fact remained: Her imagination was definitely in overdrive as she caught the faint musky scent of his body that still clung to the briefs, dealt with the heady image of them molded to his masculinity.

She was crazy. What was she doing, a supposedly liberated woman, scrubbing a man's shorts and fantasizing about them? It was their situation here, she told herself firmly. Their tantalizing Adam and Eve existence. In any other circumstances she wouldn't be experiencing this aching, dangerous longing. Or would she? Where Adam Fuller was concerned, she was no longer certain of anything.

As she finished rinsing and wringing out the last pair of socks, she decided that there was one satisfaction to be realized from this back-breaking operation. She was proving to herself that she could capably handle the rough conditions of the north country. Life in Frazer Inlet might just be a piece of cake after this.

Pleased with herself, Regan loaded the washing into a wicker basket, slipped into her coat and boots and carried the basket into the backyard. Adam had strung up a line for her in the clearing before taking off across the lake. He was going to check the conditions on the river, hoping to find that the ice there was starting to weaken.

The air outside was soft enough that Regan thought their clothes would dry before the temperature dropped after dark. She was pinning her laundry to the line when a movement out of the corner of her eye captured her attention. She turned her head to discover a young snowshoe rabbit hopping slowly along the edge of the woodshed. Her nearby presence in no way seemed to concern him.

She smiled and watched him for a minute, enchanted by the whiteness of the appealing creature, his flattened, dark-tipped ears and broad, furry feet.

She had gone back to hanging the clothes when she was startled by a flashing shadow overhead. A swoosh of powerful wings was followed almost instantly by a hideous squealing. Whipping around, she was horrified to discover that her snowshoe rabbit was struggling under the claws of a snowy owl.

Regan didn't hesitate. Dropping the garment she was holding, she flew to the aid of the rabbit. Her yells had little effect on the two creatures thrashing in the snow. The owl, hissing at her resentfully, its great wings flapping fiercely, was reluctant to release its prey. Only when she seized a stick of firewood and poked at it threateningly did it leave the rabbit and beat off into the trees.

She probably had no business interfering with nature's normal process, but Regan couldn't bear to just stand by and watch something helpless being attacked and destroyed. The owl could find another meal, one she didn't have to know about.

Dropping the stick, she knelt in the snow beside the crouched, pitiful rabbit. She was surprised when he didn't streak away from her. She thought he might be too stunned by his experience to flee, until she saw drops of blood in the snow and realized that he was injured and couldn't run.

Carefully gathering the trembling animal into her hands, she came to her feet. It was at this second that Adam, having heard the racket from below the slope and fearing the worst, trotted into the yard.

"What's wrong?" he shouted. "Are you all right?"

When he joined her by the woodshed, she showed him the rabbit and told him what had happened.

"Is that all?" he said. "I thought you were being gored by a bull moose."

"Don't be callous," she scolded. "Look at him, Adam. The poor thing is hurt."

He bent his head, inspecting the rabbit. "Owls have talons like razors. They slashed your critter's hip down here. You can believe he wouldn't have hung around and allowed you to pick him up otherwise. He's helpless until this thing heals. What are you going to do with him?"

"Well, I'm not turning him loose for some other animal's dinner. It's not fair, not when he has no defense."

"Regan, he's a wild creature. He might not survive captivity."

"I don't care," she insisted stubbornly. "I'm not letting him go until his wound is mended enough that he can manage on his own. I'll—I'll keep him in a box on the service porch where it's cool but protected. There must be some kind of box in all that junk in the storage shed. Adam, please?"

He sighed in exasperated surrender. "Take him into the house. I'll go find you your box."

When he joined her in the kitchen a moment later, bearing a small wooden crate, he found her seated on a chair trying to hang on to the rabbit who was squirming in her lap, wanting now to get away.

She looked up at him pleadingly. "The shock is worn off. He's terrified, and I'm afraid I'll only hurt him more."

Adam set the crate on the floor. "Here, give him to me." She passed the struggling rabbit into his care. "Where's that first-aid kit we brought from the plane? We ought to smear some antibiotic ointment on his wound."

"It's in the lounge. I'll get it."

When Regan came back with the tube of jell, she found the rabbit no longer in a panic. It rested quietly, trustingly in Adam's big hands as he spoke to it soothingly and gently stroked its quivering ears. The sight moved her deeply. Under this man's gruffness was a fundamental tenderness. But she had known that almost from the start.

She watched in fascination as he carefully cleaned the slashed hip and applied the ointment. "He'll probably lick it off," he said, "but maybe it will do some good."

The rabbit was settled in the deep crate and placed on a table at one end of the service porch. They stood over the table and watched the creature as it stirred slowly around the makeshift pen, investigating its new surroundings with a nose that never stopped twitching. Regan found its effort encouraging.

"What should I feed it?" she wondered.

"There's a clump of alders down along the slope. I'd try the buds and bark from those. That ought to fatten him up." He turned his head, grinning at her teasingly. "You realize we should be considering this guy in terms of food, not a pet."

She punched him in the arm. "You beast, don't even think it."

He laughed, his eyes crinkling attractively with the first sense of humor he had displayed since that unhappy morning when he had turned away from her so angrily. The tension between them was gone, and she was relieved. He was ready to be friends once more, as long as their relationship carried none of its former risk. She wondered if they both would be capable of remembering that. It wasn't going to be easy, not when a little thing such as the radial lines at the corners of his eyes could make disturbing flutters at the bottom of her stomach.

"So," he asked, "you like animals, huh?"

She smiled over the obviousness of that observation. "Passionately, to the everlasting regret of my family. I was always dragging something home that needed patching or feeding. Usually both. That's how I got Russell three years ago. He was all ribs and fleas when I found him hanging around the school playground with no one to claim him." She sighed longingly. "I guess I miss Russell more than I miss running water and central heat."

"I take it," he said dryly, "that Russell is a pooch, not a boa constrictor."

"Of course, he's a dog. A very smart dog. Mostly Irish setter."

One of his dark, heavy eyebrows arched teasingly as he eyed her hair. "Appropriately red, huh? Why Russell?"

"Why not? It seemed to fit him."

"Yeah, why not?" He cleared his throat in an exaggerated manner. "Well, since we're talking pets here I guess it's time to confess that I have a hound of my own."

"You do?" It was the first time he'd revealed anything actually personal about himself. It pleased her that he had and that they had this interest in common. "What's his name? Or is he a her?"

"Rover. And he's a him."

"Oh." It had been too much to hope for that his dog would turn out to be the elusive Jennifer. "*Rover?* Hey, real imaginative."

He grinned at her playfully again. "No, actually his name is Tex."

"Why Tex? No, don't tell me. Let me guess. It's because—"

"*—he's big like the state,*" they said in unison, both of them laughing.

"Are you being serious?" she asked. "Do you really have a Tex waiting for you?"

"Sure, in a kennel back home."

"Russell's with my parents. I'm lucky I don't have to put him into a kennel when I'm gone."

"How smart?" he challenged her, that teasing gleam still in his eyes.

"What?"

"You boasted he's a real smart dog. I just wanna know how smart."

She gazed at him suspiciously. "Is this about to be one of those my-dog-can-beat-up-your-dog kind of things?"

"Maybe," he drawled. "Come on, how smart?"

The snowshoe rabbit in his box was forgotten as they got down to the serious business of dog-bragging. Adam, arms folded across his chest and his shapely male posterior leaning back on the edge of the table, regarded her with idle confidence as he waited for her answer. Regan, one hand propped on her end of the table, eyed him in outward reluctance. Inwardly she glowed with the masculine allure of his banter.

"Well, okay. For starters, Russell fetches the newspaper for me. Automatically, in all kinds of weather."

"Uh-huh. And so can about ten million other mutts in North America. You'll have to do better than that, MacLeod."

"I said that was just for starters. There's lots else. Just let me think."

"While you're doing that, I'll tell you that Tex not only brings the paper in for me but also the mail from my box. Uses his teeth to open the lid and his nose to close it."

"Big deal. Can he catch a Frisbee in midair? Russell can."

"Not only catches it," he assured her calmly, "but tosses it back with a shake of his head. I have to admit we're still working on his accuracy."

Regan squinted at him skeptically. "Oh, come on now."

"No, it's true." He crossed his heart solemnly.

She concentrated, then suddenly remembered. "All right, all right," she said excitedly, "here's something else Russell can do—"

"Hold it." He held up his hand in a time-out signal.

"Giving up already?" she wondered gleefully.

"In your dreams. All I'm doing is calling a temporary cease-fire."

"Why?"

"I'm just thinking that if we're going to have a contest here, we need to make an occasion out of it."

"Like?"

"Maybe a party in front of the fireplace tonight. Seems to me I saw popcorn and cocoa in the pantry. What do you say?"

"All right," she agreed, "I'm up for a little entertainment. Ground rules?"

"No holds barred."

"Fine. Got a wager in mind?"

"Sure. Loser has to be the first one up out of bed in the morning to fuel both the fireplace and the kitchen stove."

"You're on, Fuller. Competition after supper dishes."

His grey eyes gleaming with mischief, he pushed away from the table and started back outdoors, calling over his shoulder a cocky, "Russell the Wonder Dog doesn't stand a chance, teacher. Not matched up against a Texas whirlwind."

"We'll see about that," she promised the rabbit as the door banged behind Adam.

Regan knew that he was going to be ready for her tonight with all kinds of fantastic exaggerations. She wasn't going to let him get away with it. She spent the rest of the day searching her imagination for extravagant claims of her own. About midafternoon, as she was making a bed of leaves in the box for the snowshoe rabbit, she suddenly realized that she was completely relaxed and having fun. The contest was just the distraction she needed. What they both needed. She understood then that this was precisely what

Adam had intended when he'd proposed the nonsensical competition.

Her opponent mysteriously disappeared just after dishes that evening, leaving her wondering what he was up to as she finished making the popcorn and cocoa. Loading a tray with their refreshments, she carried it into the lounge.

She found Adam waiting for her on the sofa drawn up in front of the fireplace. He was wearing the same faded, snug jeans he had worn earlier, but he had changed his top. This was something she had never seen before—a Houston Oilers sweatshirt. His broad shoulders wore it magnificently.

She eyed the shirt with a little smile as she placed the tray on the low table in front of the sofa. "What's this? Your Texas cheering section?"

"Yeah, something like that. What do you think?"

"I think you're going to lose."

She joined him on the sofa. For the next twenty minutes, as they munched happily on handfuls of popcorn and sipped from their steaming mugs in front of the cozy fire, they traded canine humor. Each of their wild claims was met with a dry, chuckling response:

"Oh, yeah, sure."

"Uh-huh, I really believe that one."

"What else are you going to try to sell me?"

The strain of the past few days was forgotten as they went on enjoying themselves. They never did determine a winner. Somewhere along the way the contest drifted off in another direction. Regan wasn't exactly sure how it happened. It might have been when she was telling Adam that her family didn't have quite the same appreciation for Russell's talents as she did.

"Russell is a chewer," she admitted. "For some reason, he's especially fond of electrical cords."

"He must get a real charge out of that," Adam observed with one of his straight faces.

"Never. He knows enough to pull the plugs from the outlets first. The thing is, he's damaged some of Dad's favorite power tools, my brother Joe's CD player, and my sister Midge's brand-new hair dryer. They don't understand that it's because Russell is very frustrated whenever he's ignored. I think it must be the result of an insecure puppyhood. What do you think?"

"What I think," Adam said plainly, "is that your family must be ready to kick both you and Russell out of the house."

"Oh, I don't live at home. I have my own small house I rent on the other side of town. None of us is at home anymore except Midge, who's the youngest and still in high school. But all of us seem to congregate there a lot."

"How do your parents like that?"

"Well," Regan said, munching on the last of the popcorn, "Dad complains that there is just no effective method today of keeping grown offspring out of the nest. The truth is, both Mom and Dad love it when we hang around."

"Just how many MacLeods are there?"

She counted them for him. "Andrew is the oldest. He's very serious. Then my sister Dru. Dru is a bit superior and standoffish, but terribly maternal underneath. I come next. Then Joe, who isn't serious about anything. And, of course, Midge. What can I tell you about Midge except she's a teenager?"

"And that says it all," Adam realized. "And you wouldn't trade one of them."

"Mmm," she agreed, "we're very close."

"Still," he pointed out, "you must have been willing to sacrifice all that if you were considering teaching way off in Frazer Inlet."

"I know. It—it's complicated. I guess I just felt that the time had come to test myself. I wanted to be like my Scottish ancestors, strong and independent. I grew up on all these stories about their wonderful courage. They settled in Manitoba and were wheat farmers. It was a very tough life."

She found herself telling him about her background, how her father had left the farm as a youth and settled in Winnipeg, where he had worked up to a management level in the flour industry. She had been born and raised in Winnipeg. Then her father had been transferred to Minnesota, and the whole family had relocated. But Regan had never forgotten her Canadian origins, particularly her Scottish heritage from the Manitoba prairies.

"They were such hardy people. But I'm afraid," she confided with a frown of regret, "that I'm not cut out of the same cloth."

"Why?" he demanded. "Because hardship scares you? Don't you think your ancestors were scared, too, whatever their achievements?"

"Yes, but not practically paranoidal like me. As a child, I was always afraid of new situations, new people, new experiences. I was terrified when it came time to learn to ride a two-wheeler, not to mention the year I had to change schools. Things like that."

"Why?"

"No particular reason. It's just the way I was. I outgrew a lot of it with the support of my family, but I still shelter myself too much. Sometimes I get so tired of being that way."

"Regan, I think you've been confusing courage with self-confidence. You don't lack bravery. If you did, you would never have decided to investigate Frazer Inlet."

"I suppose that could be true," she admitted, not totally convinced but warmed by his easy faith in her.

"So, why Frazer Inlet in particular? Why someplace so remote to test yourself?"

"For one thing, I've always been fascinated by the Inuit culture. I guess a part of that fascination is admiration for people who have the strength to survive in such a harsh environment."

"Like your admiration for your ancestors on the Manitoba prairies," he pointed out.

"Yes," she said. "And lately it's begun to bother me that I've just let myself drift, because I do respect people who challenge themselves to go out and try something different and exciting, which I haven't done before. Like you, for example. You know how to fly a plane. That has to be exhilarating."

"I don't know about exhilarating," he said. "Useful, yes."

"Is flying an important part of your life?" she asked, hoping to unlock at least one of his secrets.

"It's been helpful in my line of work," he answered her cautiously. "That's why I learned to pilot myself."

Construction work, she remembered. He had said something back at the plane about being involved in a construction project. "In Texas?" she wondered. She waited for him to go on, longing to have him reminisce about his own background. She should have realized he wouldn't do that. He didn't want her to know. He didn't *trust* her to know.

Regan regretted her careless probing. They had finally been comfortable with each other, and now the strain was back between them. She could feel it in his sudden silence. There was no sound now but the soft popping of the fire.

She risked a sidelong glance at Adam. He had slouched down on the sofa and was staring at the low flames, mesmerized by them. His face wore the brooding expression that by now was familiar to her, the angles of his face hardened in a mood of melancholy frustration. Her question had triggered memories he had temporarily submerged. Now he had forgotten her, forgotten his surroundings as those memories surfaced, plaguing him.

He's thinking of Jennifer, she realized. Whoever she is, he's thinking of Jennifer.

Regan didn't know why she was so certain of this, but intuition told her it was so. And she minded sharing him with Jennifer, minded more than she had any right to. She wanted to reach him, wanted him back with her. That wasn't reasonable, either. She didn't care. She just knew that she needed his closeness.

He had tried to tell her she had courage. If this was possible, then she was going to tap that courage now. She turned to him, placed a hand on his arm, and made herself ask insistently, "Do you miss her very much, Adam?"

He trained a pair of startled gray eyes on her. "What?"

"Jennifer," she persisted. "Who is she, Adam?"

A wild, trapped look came over his face. He muttered something she didn't understand, pulled away from her and surged to his feet. She watched him in unhappy bewilderment as he rounded the sofa and grabbed his coat from the back of a rocking chair.

"Where are you going?" she cried.

He didn't answer her. His long strides carried him across the lounge and out the front door. Seconds later, she could hear him on the porch pacing restlessly.

For a long moment she sat there, hating her sense of helplessness. There was stillness now on the porch. She couldn't stand not knowing what was happening out there. She got to her feet and crossed to the window. Leaning over the old, scarred console containing the windup phonograph, she pressed her face timidly to the glass.

Adam was standing rigidly at the edge of the porch, hands gripping the rustic railing, gaze directed toward the lake below. A gibbous moon swam in and out of patches of ragged cloud, defining the scene for her. The lake seemed to shimmer under the moonlight, as though it were liquid and not ice.

Adam's back was to her, but she could feel his tenseness, knew that he was staring longingly at that stretch of whiteness, as if he could will it to melt for him.

She couldn't stand his desperation, his utter aloneness. She couldn't stand not going to him. But she didn't think he would welcome her company. Then she had an inspiration.

Crouching down in front of the console, she searched through the stack of dusty, faded seventy-eights piled on the open shelf under the player. She had already experimented with the phonograph and knew that it worked.

Finding the record she wanted, she got to her feet and placed it on the turntable. She wound the crank slowly and carefully, tightening the mechanism, then positioned the needle arm over the record. Adam was too involved with his dark thoughts to hear her when she raised the window several inches.

Her action told her that maybe she was beginning to find and use the courage he insisted she had. But this knowledge didn't prevent her nervous uncertainty when she slipped out onto the porch, closing the door quietly behind her.

She stood behind him, not knowing whether he would resent her effort or accept it. Through the window, the recording a bit scratchy with age and hard use, but still true and clear, came the mellow voice of Nat King Cole and the sweet strings that accompanied him. "The Very Thought of You." Smooth, soothing, ageless.

Adam stiffened when the first strains reached him. Holding her breath, she watched him, hoping, waiting. Slowly, as the healing music poured over him, he relaxed and turned from the railing to discover her standing there.

There was no wind, but the night air was cold and she hadn't worn her coat. She was hugging herself to keep warm. The lamplight from the lounge window backlit her russet hair, turning it into a red-gold halo. He thought she was exquisite, and he had a strong urge to cherish her. Nothing more at this moment. Just cherish her.

But he didn't sound as though he felt that way when he spoke to her. His voice was sharp and gruff. "You're shivering," he accused her.

"I won't be if you hold me," she whispered. "Will you hold me, Adam? Will you dance with me?"

He hesitated. He couldn't see her face. Her face was in shadow. But he could read the expression in her voice. Soft, yearning. There was no wisdom in this. He didn't care. He opened his arms, and she came to him.

There was magic in the whole business. A corny, crazy magic. But he didn't care about that, either. He rocked her in his arms. Her body was pliant and utterly feminine against his. He bent his head, pressing his cheek to hers, feeling her silken smoothness. He liked cradling her in his arms, liked the intimacy of their bodies moving in unison.

They swayed, glided and turned across the porch. A faint breeze stirred over the roof. Flakes drifted from the eaves like a gentle snowfall. They danced with the flakes as Nat King Cole went on serenading them with the poignant "The Very Thought of You." Adam tried to forget the misery and hopelessness of his situation and didn't altogether succeed. The song was too bittersweet for that.

Maybe Regan sensed this. Maybe she felt the aching sadness that still clung to him. She lifted on tiptoe, placing her mouth against his ear, whispering an urgent, "There's something you need to know, something I've just remembered."

"What?" he whispered back. "What is it?"

She spoke the words slowly and carefully in his ear so that he couldn't mistake them. *"Russell knows how to dance."*

FREE BOOKS CERTIFICATE

Yes! Please send me **FOUR Free Silhouette Desires** together with my **Free Gifts**. Please also reserve a special Reader Service subscription for me. If I decide to subscribe, I shall receive six superb new titles every month for just £10.20 postage and packing free. If I decide not to subscribe I shall write to you within 10 days. Any free books and gifts will remain mine to keep. I understand that I am under no obligation whatsoever - I may cancel or suspend my subscription at any time simply by writing to you. *I am over 18 years of age.*

2S3SD

Name *(Mrs, Miss, Ms, Mr)* _____

Address _____

_____ Postcode _____

Signature _____

A FREE GIFT

Return this card now and we'll also send you this cuddly Teddy Bear absolutely Free together with...

A MYSTERY GIFT

We all love mysteries, so as well as the FREE books and Teddy Bear we've an intriguing Gift specially for you.

POST TODAY!

Reader Service
FREEPOST
P.O. Box 236
Croydon
CR9 9EL

NO
STAMP
NEEDED

Six

For a moment her words didn't register with him. Then he lifted his head and began to laugh. "Oh, Regan," he choked, "that's wonderful!"

She tightened her arms around him, relishing the pleasure of his hearty laughter. But in the end his easy mirth couldn't vanquish the stronger emotion under it. She was startled when his deep laughter suddenly broke on a ragged sound that was close to a sob.

He released her abruptly and stepped back. "I—I can't do this," he muttered, wiping his eyes.

She watched him struggle to regain his self-control. He had almost cried like a lost child. That very human emotion deeply touched her. But Adam, the exasperatingly strong Texas male, was ashamed of his reaction.

"It's all right," she murmured encouragingly.

"No," he said hoarsely. "No, it isn't." He grunted an impatient, frustrated sound and swung away from her.

He left her on the porch and went back into the house. She stood there until she finally realized that there was silence. The song had ended, and without Adam's warmth she was cold again.

She followed him inside. The needle was clicking softly in the end groove on the record. She crossed slowly to the phonograph, removed the record and shut the window. Then, unwilling to surrender the courage that had cost her so much effort, she went to the fireplace. He had just added new logs to the blaze. They didn't need his attention, but he was standing there poking at them savagely, as though he needed something to punish.

She watched him for a moment, and then she asked him softly, "Is it all so hopeless, Adam?"

He dropped the poker to the hearth with a clatter and turned, leaning one shoulder wearily against the mantel. She realized that for some reason the anguish was much worse for him tonight. Maybe because they had been having fun and it had suddenly struck him that it was all wrong for him to indulge himself like that. She didn't know. She only knew that she couldn't bear to see him this way, his eyes haunted, his face ravaged with a terrible despair.

He raked a hand through his dark hair, his voice raw and raspy with pain. "What do you want from me?"

"Adam," she implored, "you can't go on like this. It's tearing you apart. You've got to talk about it."

The smile he gave her was a cruel sneer. "You Scots are stubborn, aren't you? You just don't know when to quit."

"Adam, don't," she whispered.

"Don't what? Don't keep telling you no? All right, what else do I have to say to get you to finally understand that it's none of your business?"

Regan didn't mean to cry. It was so stupidly weak of her. But the tears came anyway. Bitter tears that rolled down her cheeks and leaked into the corners of her mouth with their warm saltiness.

Adam was with her at once, a groan of remorse rising from deep inside him. She found herself being held, comforted within the circle of his arms, his thick voice crooning a low plea. "Regan, don't cry. *Don't.* It's not you. It's never been you, only me. I'm a real bastard. I'm not worth it."

He didn't understand her tears. He thought they were because he had hurt her. He didn't realize that she was crying because she couldn't stand his bleakness, his fear that kept him from accepting her compassion for whatever devil was riding him.

She wanted to stop crying, but she couldn't seem to manage to achieve it. He didn't know what to do about her tears. He felt helpless and protective at the same time. He was responsible for her, like it or not. And he wanted her. God help him, but he wanted her.

His hands framed her face, lifting it to his. With all the gentleness he could summon, he brought his lips to hers, striving to kiss away her tears.

He intended the kiss to be an innocent one, a consoling one. But her mouth opened under his, welcoming him. There was just no way he could resist her invitation. His foraging tongue found hers in a slow, sweet dance. She pressed against him, deepening the kiss. He could feel the wetness of the tears on her face, could taste them. And he yearned for her.

His hands left her face and found the fullness of her breasts, stroking their soft, rounded sides, feeling their heat through the nubby sweater. And all the while he kissed her. He couldn't stop kissing her. His mouth couldn't get enough of her.

Where this long fusion, alternately tender and fierce, might have taken them he never learned. A log settled in the fireplace with a shower of sparks. The soft explosion returned them to reality. He lifted his mouth from hers with a deep, shuddering sigh of regret. Her wide, sherry-colored eyes, luminous in the firelight, searched his, seeking his mood.

He smiled down at her reassuringly. "We're a fine pair tonight, aren't we? Both of us weeping all over the place."

Regan smiled back at him, but she wasn't deceived. He was already prepared to change the subject. In another moment he would lightly dismiss the whole thing, as though it had never happened. She would lose the opportunity to reach him. She wasn't going to permit that.

"I'm not giving up on you, Adam," she promised him. "Not this time."

His arms dropped from her waist. He started to turn away from her.

She stopped him with a tremulous but emphatic, "*No,* listen to me. *Please* listen to me. You—you're protecting me. I know that's what you're doing, and it matters to me that you'd care like that. But it's wrong. If I'm ever to stand on my own two feet, everyone has to stop protecting me. *I* have to stop protecting me."

"Maybe," he said soberly, "I'm protecting myself as well."

"Is it working, Adam?" she demanded softly. "Is your silence working?"

Damn it! he thought. She knew all too well that it wasn't working, that he was living in a hell that grew worse with each day of useless waiting.

"Let me share it, Adam," she begged. "Let me understand this private nightmare of yours."

She was right. He couldn't hold out against her any longer. He did want her to know. He *needed* her to know. Maybe that need was just a fundamental human desire to unburden himself of a thing that was intolerable. Or maybe it was for another reason that he wasn't ready to confront. Either way, he feared her judgment.

"I'm not the only one struggling for courage, am I?" she asked him, realizing his indecisiveness.

He shook his head slowly. "I guess not," he admitted.

Regan knew then that he was going to tell her. She tried to make it as easy for him as possible. She went and sat down in the rocking chair away from the distraction of being too close to him. The chair creaked and wobbled as she settled in it, but after that she kept it very still. She placed her feet firmly on the floor, her hands in her lap, and she waited quietly for him to begin.

Her eyes followed him as he wandered restlessly around the lounge, aimlessly picking up Indian artifacts, turning them in his hands and then replacing them. He began to talk to her in a voice that was carefully even, as though he feared his intense emotions over the subject.

"Houston," he said. "That's home for me. Do you know Houston?"

Regan shook her head. "No, I've never been there."

"It's a great city, though I haven't spent my whole thirty-six years in it. I was born and raised on a ranch near Lubbock. Well, not much of a ranch. Pretty poor by Texas standards and mortgaged to the hilt. I got out after my folks died. I spent some years bumming around the country, mostly working in construction. I learned the business and found out that I liked it. When I went back to Texas, I settled in Houston. The town was booming in those days. I wanted to get in on the expansion. I started my own construction business. Just a small outfit. I was struggling to get it off the ground when I met Valerie."

Valerie, Regan thought. Not the elusive Jennifer. Not yet.

"I was taking night courses at a local college," he went on. "Subjects that I thought would help me with my business. Valerie was in one of my classes. I noticed her right away. Valerie was the kind of woman you did notice. Pretty sensational. At least that's what I thought back then. We started going out together. It was all so quick. It just seemed overnight to go from casual to serious, and before I knew it we weren't just talking marriage, we *were* married."

Regan remembered his telling her back at the derelict houseboat that he'd had a wife and that he'd lost her.

"We were young," Adam explained, "and I guess we were awfully impulsive. Looking back, I can see that I didn't really know her. I thought she wanted the same solid things out of life I wanted. I didn't understand that what Valerie was really looking for was a kind of sexual excitement. Apparently it was there for her in the early years when I was still doing a lot of the heavy construction labor myself. That's what appealed to Valerie, the earthy, macho stuff.

"It started to go wrong for us as I got more successful with the business. Oh, she appreciated the money that was beginning to come in, but she was also bored by my new identity. I was no longer this virile, sweating brute for her, just an ordinary businessman. It doesn't make sense, but that's how she was."

"Were you still in love with her?" Regan asked.

Adam shook his head. "I'm not sure I ever was in love with her. Maybe all the time it was just a physical attraction."

"Did you separate?"

"We should have. Only there was Jennifer. The best thing that ever happened to me. For Jennifer's sake, I wanted to keep the marriage together."

Jennifer, Regan thought. Jennifer at last. And as he spoke of her, there was the first real emotion in his voice. The deep emotion of a loving, caring father. Because, of course, Jennifer was his daughter.

Restraining her surprise, Regan asked a level, "How old?"

"Jenny's almost nine now. You probably know that age."

"Very well."

"Anyway, I wanted the best for her. I wanted her to have what kids are supposed to have. A secure home and family. What you had growing up with your folks, Regan."

"And that wasn't possible," she said with realization.

He spread his hands in a gesture of helplessness. "Valerie was having affairs. She was always careful about them, but I knew what was happening. In the end—well, I just couldn't keep turning my back and pretending. That's when I realized that our staying together was hurting Jenny, not helping her. We were in the process of divorcing when—when Valerie died."

Regan sensed what was coming. She gripped her hands together in her lap and held herself very steady in the rocking chair. She knew she was about to hear a cruel tragedy and that it was crucial she receive it without the shock and the horror that would make him regret confiding in her. It wasn't physical danger that tested real courage. She understood that now. Among other things, real courage was having nonjudgmental faith in the people you cared for. She was ready for that test.

Adam was no longer moving around the room. He was back at the fireplace, watching her with a kind of challenge in his eyes. "She was murdered, Regan," he told her woodenly. "Valerie was murdered, and they think I did it."

There was silence in the room except for the slow hiss of resin escaping from one of the burning logs. He waited for her reaction. Her response was vital to him.

"What happened?" she asked him calmly. "Tell me everything that happened."

The hardness around his jaw softened, relaxed now that he knew she wasn't going to cringe from him. She could take what he had to reveal.

He looked down into the fire, shaking his head slowly. "It looks bad for me. About as bad as it could look. I had both the motive and the opportunity, you see, so everything points to my having done it. It—it's all pretty brutal."

"Go on," she urged him.

"Like I said," he continued, still gazing at the fire, "we were in the process of the divorce. I'd moved out of the house and was living in a rented condo. We—well, relations between us were strained and our meetings weren't friendly ones. In fact, they were downright hostile. Valerie was being vindictive about the whole thing. She meant to have a big settlement out of me, as well as custody of Jennifer."

"And you were fighting that?"

"That's what her friends and neighbors thought. And that's what they told the police. Hell, they had every reason to believe it's what our shouting matches were all about, and it suited Valerie to let them believe it. See, I was in a tight spot financially, and everyone knew that. Houston's economy hasn't been good lately, and my business was suffering for it. But then this project came along, an office complex, and it looked like everything could turn around for me. The thing is, it meant tying up all my funds."

"And Valerie threatened that," Regan said.

"Yeah, she threatened it. But that isn't what we were battling about. Hell, I don't care about the money. Not to that extent. It was only Jennifer I cared about. My little girl was at risk, and I was furious over that."

"Your daughter was—I don't understand."

"Valerie had a new man in her life. When she was feeling spiteful, and that happened all the time at the end, she taunted me about him. Boasting how exciting a lover he was, everything she considered I wasn't. She wouldn't tell me much about him, other than that. Afraid I might use it against her, I guess. But she let slip enough that I got the picture. He was an oil rigger, one of those rough, mean types she went for like a sickness. God only knows where she met him. Maybe in a bar. She did mention he was off one of the Gulf rigs, and bars are the first place some of those guys head for when they hit town."

"And Jennifer saw her mother and this man—"

"No." Adam shook his head vigorously. "Thank God, no. Valerie managed to keep him a secret. She wasn't about to do anything that would jeopardize that settlement she wanted. As far as I know, no one knew about the guy but me. And as for my knowing at all...well, I guess she figured her word was as good as mine, because I'd have no witnesses, no evidence."

"Then why were you—"

"Worried about Jennifer? It was because Valerie mentioned in one of her nastier moments that her boyfriend was going up to work in a new oil field that had just opened on Hudson Bay. As soon as the divorce was final, she intended to follow him, and she meant to take Jenny with her.''

"Frazer Inlet," Regan said on a soft breath of understanding.

He nodded. "Frazer Inlet, yes. I was wild over that. Not just for all the obvious reasons, either. This oil rigger of hers was the abusive type. Val would never admit that, but she had some bruises on her. I knew where they came from. No way was I going to stand for my little girl being in a situation like that. We had a bad scene over it. The neighbors heard me yelling warnings at her. They just didn't know the facts behind those warnings.''

"But the bruises she carried—"

"Yeah, the bruises." Adam laughed, a dry, bitter laugh. "Her friends and neighbors thought I was responsible for those. Valerie blamed them on me in order to win sympathy for her divorce demands. It was one more thing against me when—when she was killed like that.''

He stopped, gazing at her anxiously from his position near the fire. She could see he was reluctant again, unwilling to give her the unpleasant details of Valerie's murder. But Regan wasn't going to let him shield her from any of the hard truth.

"Tell me the rest," she demanded. "How did she die?''

She watched his Adam's apple bobbing as he swallowed through the emotional tightness in his throat. And then he told her. "I went by the house late one evening to try to talk to Valerie one last time. I was willing by then to give her anything she asked, but I wanted Jennifer. I was hoping to persuade her to give me custody of our daughter, and she could have the rest. I thought it was a good time to see her, because I knew Jenny was staying overnight with a friend. I never wanted Jenny to see those angry scenes between her mother and me.''

"Did you talk to her?''

Adam shook his head. "No. The house was dark and the door was locked. I still had my own key, but I didn't see any point in going in. I figured she was out somewhere with her oil rigger. I was mad about that and frustrated because she wasn't there. The next door neighbor saw me driving away in an agitated state. The woman told the police afterward that she felt I might have been threatening Valerie again, and she was worried about her. Val had given her a key to the house because she was always misplacing hers. The woman went over there to check on her. She found Valerie's battered body in the bedroom. She'd been dead less than an hour. Beaten and strangled in a murderous rage. It—it was still around her throat."

"What?" Regan whispered.

"The necktie. One of my own neckties that I'd left behind when I moved out of the house."

"Oh, dear God," Regan said, clapping a horrified hand to her mouth.

Adam smiled at her crookedly. It was the most desolate smile she had ever seen. "Yeah, it all came back to me," he said, his voice husky with anguish. "Every bit of it. The motive, my anger over the situation that amounted to desperation, the fact that I had no alibi, that I'd even been seen at the damn house that night. All of it came back against me."

Regan stared at him, knowing how vital the moment was. If she failed to believe him now when no one else did, if she turned away from him in fear, then she would lose forever the trust she was striving to win from him. But that wasn't going to happen, because not for a second did Regan doubt anything he had told her. She leaned forward tensely in the rocking chair, her voice clear and unwavering.

"But it's all circumstantial evidence. The police must realize that."

She caught a flicker of gratitude in his gray eyes. He didn't fully comprehend yet that she was accepting his innocence without question, that she was completely on his side. But he was relieved she wasn't regarding him with the distaste and suspicion of everyone back in Houston.

His broad shoulders lifted in a small shrug. "Maybe that's why I wasn't arrested right away. But they questioned me plenty. Oh, how they questioned me, again and again." His voice turned shaky with pain. "What hurt the most is that anyone would believe I could be capable of murdering the mother of my daughter, whatever I thought about her."

"The oil rigger," she said. "You're convinced it was the oil rigger, aren't you?"

He nodded. "Who else? Valerie hadn't been robbed, the house hadn't been broken into. Whoever did it was someone she knew and let in, which is another fact that's against me."

"It had to have been the oil rigger," Regan insisted. "You said he was an abusive, mean type. It all fits, and if he had an explosive temper— But murder, that's extreme. What would drive him to that?"

He shook his head. "I don't know. Valerie could be difficult. No one knows that better than me. She could push a man to his limits. Maybe this guy didn't want a permanent relationship, her following him to Canada with her kid. But if she pressed him, got ugly about it . . . I just don't know."

"What did the police say about this man?" Regan wanted to know. "Didn't they bring him in, question him?"

"They didn't believe me," Adam said. "They think he's someone I invented. Oh, they conducted the usual investigation, of course, talked to all of Valerie's friends and neighbors, but no one had ever seen him or remembered hearing her mention him. She'd managed to keep her Ricky a secret from all of them."

"*Ricky?*" Regan fastened on the name. "Valerie actually told you his name?"

"Just that one pet name and only once when she was being careless."

"But if you have his identity—"

"It hasn't helped much, Regan. Not back in Houston. Believe me, I wasn't standing still. I was trying myself to locate this guy. I went to some of the oil riggers when the police released me after that first questioning. I tried to talk to them, but they're a clannish lot, suspicious as hell. It didn't help that the police had gotten to them first. If they knew anything about one of their buddies, they weren't admitting it. I finally bribed one old fellow who said that maybe there had been a guy the girls called Ricky and that maybe, just maybe, he had slipped out of town to go off and work in the oil fields at Frazer Inlet, though he wouldn't swear to any of it. But it was all I had to go on."

"So you went to Frazer Inlet to find him yourself?"

"I had to," Adam said. "I was frantic by then. My lawyer felt that the police were ready to arrest me and charge me for Valerie's murder. I knew I didn't stand a chance if that happened, not if everyone was already convinced I'd killed her to save my business from going under."

"Adam," she said gently, "shouldn't you have—well, hired a professional?"

His shoulders hunched again in angry despair. "Private detectives cost the earth, and my funds were all tied up in that building project. Besides, nobody was trusting me by then, so I was afraid to trust anyone in return." He made an impatient gesture with his hands. "Okay, maybe it was a mistake. Maybe my running off like that is only going to convince them that I have to be guilty. But all I could think about was finding this guy and making him talk. I wasn't going to sit there and wait to be arrested. I was going to help myself. I left Jenny with Valerie's sister and grabbed the first plane out of Houston."

"What happened in Frazer Inlet?"

He shook his head. "Nothing. Nobody up there knew anything about him. I would have gone on searching, but the Mounties must have received a bulletin on me. They came for me, notified Houston, and—Well, you know the rest."

Regan edged forward on the rocking chair. "What will you do now?"

"Stay free," he vowed. "I've got to stay free until I get this guy. I've got to go on looking."

"For your daughter's sake as well as your own," she said. "That's why, isn't it?"

His mouth tightened to a line of grim resolve. "Jennifer's already lost one parent. If I go to prison, she'll end up losing both of us. She'll have no one but Valerie's sister. Kate is all right, but she's totally career-involved. She can never be what Jenny needs."

Regan understood everything now. He had been sick with worry over Jennifer, uncompromising on her behalf. His every tough action, his every harsh mood had been the result of his need to safeguard his daughter. She understood, and her heart ached for him in his desperation.

She watched him, seeing his shoulders suddenly slump. He had told her everything, drained himself. He circled around the sofa and settled on its low arm, pressing his thumb and forefinger against the appealing hump in his nose. For a moment he looked down at the floor. And then he lifted his gaze, smiling at her thinly.

"Maybe they're right," he said tiredly. "Maybe this oil rigger doesn't exist, and I'm chasing a phantom."

Regan couldn't stand his desolation. He'd been alone through all of this, suffering every awful bit of it entirely on his own. She wasn't going to permit him to go on fighting alone.

She didn't hesitate. She pushed up from the rocking chair and went to the sofa, dropping to her knees in front of him. Leaning forward with his forearms resting on his strong thighs, his hands were dangling between his legs. She grasped them in her own hands, hanging on to them tightly.

"You're not wrong," she insisted, her voice fierce with determination. "He *does* exist, and someone somewhere must know where he is. We'll have to find him, Adam. We'll have to trace him."

"We?" The handsome gray eyes searched her face, discovering in her expression the unyielding obstinacy of her forefathers.

"Yes, *we.*"

He went on looking at her with uncertainty, but her stubbornness never faltered. His last, lingering inability to trust her left him in the face of the emphatic support she was offering without question. He could fully accept now her belief in his story, her complete faith in his innocence. And he was shaken by it. He had never had a woman's simple caring confidence in him that asked nothing in return. He was grateful for it, even awed by it, but he didn't know how to respond to it.

"Aw, Regan," he muttered unhappily, "do you think I'd involve you in this mess any more than I have already? That isn't why I told you. I told you because . . ." He trailed off, leaving the rest unsaid.

"Because you couldn't stand it anymore," she finished for him softly, gazing encouragingly into his lean face above hers. "There was no one to believe in you, and you needed someone to listen and believe. Don't you think I see and understand that? But now you have that someone."

"No." he insisted. "You don't know what you're saying. You'd be at risk if you tried to help me. Do you think I want that?"

He tried to withdraw his hands, but she clung to them. "I'm here for you, Adam," she said, appealing to him earnestly. "Let me be here for you. Use me. There must be some way I can help. Together we can figure out a way."

"I don't know." He shook his head. "I just don't know."

"We'll talk about it," she promised. "Later we'll talk about it, plan what we have to do."

His hands lay limply now in hers. For the moment, anyway, the resistance had been burned out of him. Perhaps it was unfair of her to take advantage of that fact, but she was on her knees between his hard thighs. She was touching him, feeling the heat of his hands linked with hers, experiencing all the significance of his vital nearness. She recognized then how much she cared about him, how much she wanted him.

She looked down and was moved by the sight of their hands together, hers slim and pale and feminine, his big and masculine and much darker by contrast. She lowered her head and rubbed her cheek slowly against the back of one of his hands still folded between hers. The black hair that grew there in little whorls felt nicely rough against her sensitive skin. It was a wonderful hand, strong and well shaped.

He didn't try to stop her when she turned one hand, pressing her mouth lovingly into the callused palm, planting a lingering kiss. The tip of her tongue traced the breadth of his hand, then caressed the length of his fingers one by one. She could taste him now, something slightly salty and tantalizingly male.

Adam caught his breath as she went on fondling him. Whether she consciously realized it or not, she was seducing him. It was a wildly provocative business, and he should be opposing it. He *needed* to oppose it. She didn't know what she was getting into. She didn't understand that it was a crazy time for this to be happening, all wrong. Something they would probably both regret afterward.

But he didn't care. He just plain didn't care. He was worn-out with tormenting himself over her alluring nearness. He didn't want to hold out any longer. He *couldn't* hold out. His need for her was too deep, too strong. And whatever that might mean, wherever it might take them— well, all that would keep and be sorted out later. Because right now...

Regan's breath sharpened when Adam's hands stirred in hers. Suddenly she was no longer clasping them. His fingers had curled around hers, wrapping over her own hands possessively, forcefully. She found herself being dragged up to his level, his powerful thighs clamped against her sides, holding her securely. His face was now only a breath away from hers.

"I wonder if you know," he whispered, his voice slow and husky, "exactly how much I've been wanting you since we stumbled out of that plane."

"That long ago?" she teased him, staring into the smoky-gray eyes holding hers.

"Yeah," he growled, "that long ago."

"Show me," she boldly challenged him.

He complied by sloping his mouth over hers in a long, enticing kiss. She could feel his raw desire in every nuance of that union: his lips branding hers, his tongue thrusting lustfully inside her mouth, his warm breath inhaling her. Regan felt as if all her senses were being stroked at once.

Tugging her hands free, she slid her fingers through the thick hair at the back of his head, locking him against her, steadying herself with his strength. There was a wanton hunger in his mouth that scalded her, that made her light-headed with the pleasure his brazen tongue invoked.

The pine resin in the fire bubbled and purred with a steamy moistness that was a counterpoint to the textures of their kiss. The blaze was incandescent, searing. Not just something apart from her, Regan realized, but inside her as well. A heat ignited by Adam's aggressive mouth plundering hers.

She had to struggle for air when he finally took pity on her and lifted his mouth from hers. She was still raised high on her knees as he leaned over her, but she would have collapsed on the floor if his arms hadn't been supporting her.

"Any doubts?" he demanded, his deep voice as raspy as a file.

"Absolutely none," she gasped.

They gazed at each other for a long, heart-stopping minute while Regan's pulse raced out of control. The unspoken plea in his eyes was unmistakable.

Her hand was trembling when she placed it against his cheek. "Does this mean," she softly teased him again, "that you're going to move your mattress back in here next to mine?"

The slow, lazy smile on his wide mouth utterly transformed him, lifting him out of his darkness and making her glow simply by his existence. "No," he drawled, "it means, teacher, I'm taking both twin mattresses upstairs and exchanging them for a double. But at this particular minute..."

Seven

At this particular minute what he wanted to do was make uninhibited, prolonged love to her. Without delay.

The fire spoke to them again, sizzling like his insides as Adam slithered off the sofa arm. Dropping to his knees, he faced her on the floor. He was still smiling as he slowly peeled the Oilers sweatshirt over his head, tossing it behind him.

Regan's breath quickened at the riveting sight of him. He was wearing nothing underneath. She marveled at the sinewy breadth of his chest with its wedge of dark, curling hair that narrowed to a fine line at the point of his navel before flaring again as it disappeared teasingly under his belt line.

Catching her hands, Adam pressed them to the hard wall of his chest. "Touch me, sweetheart," he commanded, his voice husky with yearning.

Her flattened palms felt the heat of his bronzed flesh. Fingers stirring, she explored the contours of his wide shoulders, then the slabs of pectoral muscle earned by years of heavy construction work. He was an awesome evidence of healthy masculinity.

Her fingers drifted on through the springy black hair, circling his nipples that were like a pair of flat buttons.

"There," he insisted. "Touch me there."

Experimentally, fearing she would hurt him, she lightly pinched both nipples. He inhaled sharply through clenched teeth, weaving on his knees.

"Yeah," he said roughly, "like that. Only harder. Much harder."

Her thumbs and forefingers exerted pressure, slowly and tightly squeezing. Head back, eyes closed, he groaned softly, the cords on his neck straining with his pleasure. The fire hissed like an indrawn breath.

"It feels good," he moaned. "It feels so good."

"Am I—"

"No," he assured her quickly, sensing her concern. "It isn't that kind of pain. I like it."

His male nipples, hard and erect, were a dark red now with the blood surging through them.

"Go down," he directed. "Touch me lower."

Her hands descended on his chest, encountering over his left ribs a white ridge of scar tissue. She caressed the old wound, regretting the pain it must have cost him.

Eyes still closed, he smiled in memory. "Had a little misunderstanding with an ornery tie beam about twelve years ago," he explained.

Dipping her head, Regan kissed the scar, soothing it with her lips and tongue.

Adam chuckled. "On the other hand, the eventual result makes that old argument kind of worthwhile." He sucked in another mouthful of air as her tongue went on laving the area. "Oh, sweetheart," he warned, "if you keep doing that..."

But Regan had no intention of withdrawing. Her mouth trailed in the direction of his navel, swirling around the deep indentation, tasting the musky, hair-roughened skin as the fire in the grate curled and licked at the logs.

"Wait," he said hoarsely. "I want to—yeah, that's it."

She raised obediently as, with trembling, impatient hands, he fumbled at his belt. Unclasping it, he snapped open his jeans, then spread the material wide. Through the gap, rising from a dark thicket, sprang the blatant evidence of his arousal, rigid and pulsing.

Thrusting towards her, Adam guided her hand to his hardness. Her fingers closed around him, stroking what felt to her like satin over steel. From low in his throat rumbled animal sounds of deep satisfaction.

Unable to bear the pleasure she was giving him, he swayed against her weakly, burying his mouth in the hollow of her throat. She held him, both of them still on their knees, as he pressed kisses along her collarbone. He wanted more of her than her sweater and shirt would permit. He wanted to please her as she pleased him. He eagerly helped her to strip away her sweater and top, to rid her of her bra.

When she was freed of the last garment, she faced him shyly. Adam, drawn back slightly, spent a long moment simply enjoying the sight of her. The firelight glinted in her tumbled russet hair, reddened her parted lips and flushed cheeks, cast a rosy glow over the fullness of her breasts with their tightly puckered buds.

"You're beautiful," he whispered, lightly touching her silky skin. "You are a beautiful woman."

"Adam—"

"Shh." He hushed her, ducking his head. "Let me...just let me..." The words were lost as his mouth closed over one of her nipples, tugging strongly.

The sensation of his wet mouth on her breast, with both his hands splayed possessively over her rib cage, made her almost sick with longing.

"Adam," she gasped, clenching his hard shoulders, "I've never felt—it's never—*ohhh*—"

Without pity, his marauding tongue went on performing a sensual torment, drawing each peak deep into his mouth. Unable to bear his wanton suckling, she sagged against him limply. He lifted his head then, but the relief he gave her was very brief.

Regan, eyes closed in a mindless haze of joy, heard the low table in front of the sofa scraping across the floor as Adam shoved it out of the way with a free hand while he supported her around the waist with his other arm. Not bothering with her nearby mattress, he lowered her to the soft Indian rug spread in front of the hearth, then stretched his length beside her. With quick, supple movements he dragged off his shoes and socks and jeans, kicking them away. Then he disposed of the rest of her clothing. Gathering her into his arms, he began kissing her again, slowly this time and with infinite tenderness.

The flickering fire gilded the naked flesh of their entwined bodies; his stalwart and lean with his maleness, hers softly rounded and vulnerable with femininity. As they squirmed in their embrace, seeking a tighter closeness with each other, the firelight shimmered over them, bathing them in a radiance of liquid gold.

The sinuous flames blinded Regan, scorched her senses so that she was unable to hear the raspy endearments Adam crooned at her ear between his long, leisurely kisses. But she was able to understand their loving intent, was able to respond to his hand slipping between her thighs to seek the source of her womanhood. She felt a heat more intense than the fire as his gentle fingers squeezed and rubbed. She undulated against him with little cries, pleading for him, feeling raw and incomplete without his swollen fullness inside her.

"Now, Adam," she begged him in urgency. "Please, now."

"Yes, sweetheart," he promised, positioning himself between her parted legs, "now."

Tremors rocked through her as she felt his probing arousal sliding against her softness, forcing through her moist, quivering petals. Then he was inside her, thrusting deep and hard, melding his flesh with hers.

She clamped her legs and arms around him, holding him tightly in a fierce ownership. She felt his back muscles constricting under her hands as he moved against her, sending jolt after jolt through her with his powerful rhythms that she struggled to answer.

Jets of flame fluttered and twisted over the pine logs, lifting and descending in noisy little spurts, a fiery accompaniment that cast a rosy sheen over their bodies glistening now with the sweat of their writhing union.

Was it her imagination, or did the blaze quicken with them? She sensed it consuming itself, thought she heard a pair of logs flaring explosively in a shower of sparks, then collapsing in a bed of searing coals. Or was it only Adam and her? Adam, who with one final massive stroke, shuddered against her as he found his release with a lusty, guttural cry. She followed almost immediately, sobbing into his shoulder as the sweet spasms raged through her.

He held her protectively as the waves slowly subsided. Then, they sank into the drowsy, mellow aftermath of utter fulfillment.

The fire was a bed of charred log ends and smoldering gray ashes when Regan stirred in the first pearly light of daybreak. Exhausted from their long bout of lovemaking, neither of them had bothered to get up during the night to feed fresh wood to the blaze. It didn't matter. She was snug and warm under the layers of blankets they shared, though neither she nor Adam wore a stitch of clothing.

They had spent the night side by side on the double mattress he had promised. He had insisted on hauling it down from an upstairs bedroom and spreading it in front of the fireplace. Then he had made love to her again before they had settled down for the night.

Regan was conscious now of his warm nearness, of being trapped under one of his muscular, hair-roughened legs, which was hooked possessively around her own leg. Smiling contentedly, she turned her eyes toward the figure close beside her, watching him as he slept.

He was on his stomach, his head turned toward her. The thick, dark hair she loved was all mussed and spiky, there was a heavy shadow of beard on his jaw and his mouth was slightly parted as he breathed with soft, even snores.

The sight of him this way, all sleepy and sexy, made her insides churn. And when she remembered last night, she went positively weak. Valerie Fuller must have been mentally unbalanced not to have appreciated this man. No male could be more virile, more desirable.

Regan caught her breath with the wonder of her conviction. The sound must have disturbed him. With a little grunt he opened his eyes and found her looking at him.

"What?" he asked with a lazy smile.

"Your nose," she promptly informed him.

"That's the first thing you greet me with? What's wrong with my nose?"

"It interests me. Well, this bump here does anyway." She lifted one finger, slowly fondling the hump on the bridge of his nose.

"Another souvenir," he explained. "This one from a fist. I used to box a little when I was young and unwise. I had it straightened once, and then it was broken again. After that I gave up on it."

"Uh-huh," she drawled.

He squirmed a bit as her gaze went on appraising him. "This is getting to be a habit, isn't it, teacher?"

"What?"

"Your examining me like this every morning."

"And you look terribly self-conscious about it, too," she teased. "It really bothers you, doesn't it?"

"No, it just amazes me you'd find anything about this mug worth looking at."

"Oh, I promise you," she assured him softly, "it is definitely worth looking at."

He grinned at her, a slow, lethargic grin that made her stomach churn again. "C'mere," he commanded roughly.

As he turned on his side, he pulled her into his arms, cradling her close. So, he was a morning cuddler. She liked that. She liked it very much.

"Now," he instructed her, rocking her gently, "if anyone around here deserves to be stared at it isn't me. Hell, I've been staring since Frazer Inlet."

"Liar. You weren't even aware of me back at Frazer Inlet."

"I was aware of you all right. From the minute I stepped out of that car I was aware of you."

"Only as a nuisance maybe."

"No, much more than that," he said, his voice smoky with a slumberous desire.

"Proof is in the action, Fuller."

A telltale hardness straining against her stomach told her that he was fully prepared to answer her challenge. No hesitation this time, no preliminaries. He took her quickly and urgently, burying his heat deep inside her, his strokes powerful and sure. In the cold gray dawn Regan cried out in rapture.

It was full daylight, the morning sun streaming through the lounge windows, when Regan awakened again. Adam, beside her, was still soundly asleep. She was too restless to go on lying there this time. But it was a good restlessness, the energy that comes from exhilaration.

She didn't stop to explain this state of being to herself. Careful not to disturb Adam, she slid out from under the blankets. The room was sharply chill, and she shivered as she snatched up her clothing and struggled into it. She stirred the fire and added fresh logs. When she was satisfied that the new wood had caught, she replaced the screen.

Then with a last tender glance at the man who continued to sleep in exhaustion, she crept away to the kitchen.

She wanted to be alone for a few minutes. She needed time to think about this joyous excitement that was racing through her veins. But her mind was all in a fluttery turmoil, refusing reason, as she busied herself in the kitchen. She made a fire in the wood stove, heated water on the kerosene range and treated herself to a quick wash. When she had changed into fresh clothes, she faced the task of making breakfast. She wanted to prepare as large and satisfying a meal as their supplies would permit. She was sure Adam would be as hungry as she suddenly was.

A moment later she caught herself standing helplessly in the middle of the kitchen and grinning like a silly fool at the prospect of facing him across the table, of sharing with him a simple, ordinary breakfast. But she still didn't admit to herself what was ailing her.

She was heading for the pantry when she remembered the snowshoe rabbit. Breakfast could wait until she had checked on him. Hoping he had survived the night, she hurried out to the enclosed service porch and peered worriedly into the box on the table.

The creature greeted her like an old friend, stretching up the side of the box, his nose twitching at her in welcome. Regan chuckled in relief. He was positively frisky, and she could see that the wound on his hip was clean and already starting to heal.

"Well, good morning to you, too. No, you can't get out yet. But real soon, I promise. Just hang in there, and you'll be hopping back to your girlfriend before you know it. You've upset your water, huh? Hold on."

She went back to the kitchen and got him a fresh saucer of water. Then she talked to him again as she fed him alder twigs from the supply she had on the table.

"So, what's new this morning, Peter Rabbit? Not much, huh? Me? Oh, the usual. You know, keeping the fires going, cooking, cleaning up. Yep, all that Cinderella stuff.

Well, one more thing. There's this guy—you know, the one who pretended to be grumpy about it when he helped you out yesterday—well, it seems I've gone and fallen head over heels in love with him. That's right, Peter, I've—''

Regan stopped with a sudden breathlessness that caught her like a blow in the ribs. This was it! This was the explanation for her wild happiness this morning! The exhilaration she had been reluctant to admit until she had casually, crazily confessed it to a snowshoe rabbit!

She leaned against the table, feeling suddenly weak with the awesome realization. It hadn't been just sex then! She was in love, *deeply* in love, with Adam Fuller!

"Now, how did that go and happen?" she mumbled to the animal. "What a shock!" But a nice shock, she thought, glowing inside. Oh, a *very* nice one.

She put her hands down to stroke the creature's flattened ears, and then she paused, listening. In the sudden silence she heard the slow, steady drip of water. Her gaze lifted to the bank of windows that went all the way to the ceiling. She could see through the glass long icicles suspended from the eaves of the porch. They were melting in the morning sun. A mounting warmth that any day now would carry the ice out of the lake and river.

It was ending. It was all coming to an end. Soon, very soon now, there would be no reason for them to stay on here. They could leave, they could go back to the outside world. And what then? Adam must find the oil rigger, of course, must clear himself. She refused to believe he wouldn't somehow. But his future was uncertain. It alarmed her to think there might not be a place in it for her.

It was so foolishly ironic. Less than twenty-four hours ago she had longed to get away from this place, to be rescued so that she could return to her home and family. Now she didn't want to leave. She wanted their isolated, magic togetherness to go on and on. But she was being selfish. Adam had a murder charge hanging over his head that had to be resolved, a daughter who needed him. He had to go back, and she had to go with him. She was certain he would want her with him. She wouldn't permit herself to consider the possibility that he might not feel about her as she felt about him. What had been between them last night was too strong, too direct to be anything but mutual love. Then why was she so frightened?

Regan stared down at the rabbit, a sudden panic clawing at her. "Oh, Peter," she confessed plaintively to the animal as he nibbled at an alder twig, "now that I've found him I can't lose him! I love him too much for that!"

Caught up in her emotions, she wasn't aware of Adam's appearance in the kitchen doorway behind her. In any case, his arrival just seconds before had been a soundless one. He was barefoot. When he had awakened and come in search of Regan, he hadn't bothered with anything but jeans and a woolen plaid shirt, still unbuttoned and hanging open over his naked chest.

He was glad now his feet were bare. It permitted him to back noiselessly away from the doorway, to turn and sneak like a coward out of the kitchen. As though he had never been there, as though he had never heard her fervent outpouring.

Adam went back to the lounge where he circled endlessly, dealing with his own panic as he nervously combed his fingers through his tousled hair.

Oh, Lord, what had he gone and done? What had he let himself in for with last night's reckless intimacy? Bad enough that he had taken her with wild abandon, without any consideration for the consequences, but he had never reckoned on this!

He wished he'd never overheard her declaration. He didn't want her to be in love with him. It shook him to the core. He didn't trust a woman's love, *any* woman's. He didn't doubt Regan's sincerity, but he was afraid of it. He was even more afraid of his own feelings. Valerie had been a painful lesson, and to risk his heart again... No, he just didn't trust it.

It was an impossible situation, and he was a bastard for allowing it to happen. He was even worse than that because now he couldn't handle it. He couldn't offer her what she deserved. And she would be hurt, deeply hurt. Unlike Valerie or any of the faceless women who had paraded through his life, Regan was decent and vulnerable. He didn't want her hurt. He cared about her too much.

But it was hopeless. Even if he had the courage to return her love, it was hopeless. He faced a murder conviction, a long sentence in prison. If he managed to get out of it somehow, and the odds were against that, it still meant a long separation for them while he fought to establish his innocence. A separation that was imminent and inevitable, waiting only on the turn of the weather.

What was he going to do? What could he say to make her understand?

He still had no answers, only a frenzied desperation tearing at his insides when Regan found him minutes later prowling around the lounge. She was in too carefree a mood, her optimism recovered, to notice the trapped look in his eyes. But she did notice his bare feet and the open, red plaid shirt that made her breath sharpen with the potent glimpse of his hard, hair-darkened chest.

"What are you doing wandering around half-dressed on these cold floors?" she demanded. "You look like a lumberjack courting pneumonia."

He couldn't help it. He resented her reproof, even though he knew she meant it strictly in a playful sense. But her concern scared him, as if she were already exercising some partner's right to criticize him.

"What do you want?" he grumbled.

She chose to overlook his scowl. "I just came to tell you I have breakfast underway, but you've got time for a shave and a wash."

"All right, I'll be out in a minute."

A cheerful sunshine was slanting across the kitchen table when they settled opposite each other twenty minutes later.

Adam was freshly shaved and fully dressed. She caught the clean fragrance of soap on him and thought how appealing he looked. But then he always appealed to her, either as scrubbed as this with his hair still damp where he had tamed it with a wet comb, or unshaven and mussed.

She resisted the proprietary urge to cover his big hand reaching for the sugar. This was terrible! It wasn't enough for her just to be close to him. She wanted to touch him as well, caress him, as if to assure herself of his existence, as if only with physical contact could she actually share him. Love, she decided, was worse than a sickness. Or maybe it *was* a kind of sickness.

"I wanted to make fresh eggs and bacon for breakfast," she apologized. "Instead, here we are eating the usual powdered stuff."

"Doesn't matter," he said, tasting his coffee and then adding another pinch of sugar. He was uncomfortably aware of her gaze lingering on him. He wished she wouldn't look at him in that manner, her eyes filled with love as plain as a headline. It made him feel rotten, a real heel.

Regan went on considering him over her glass of powdered orange juice. Should she tell him how she felt? She longed to tell him. No, it was too soon. Besides, she was just starting to realize through her dazed happiness that he was in a strange mood, one that didn't invite confidences.

She put down her orange juice. "Something wrong?" she asked.

"No," he denied, avoiding her gaze as he poured powdered milk over his oatmeal.

He wasn't going to refer to last night then, she realized. Oh, God, did he regret it? She couldn't stand the pang of that possibility. But the fact remained, he was definitely remote with her when only an hour ago...

Jennifer, she thought suddenly, grasping at an explanation. Maybe he was worried again about Jennifer. That would be understandable. She wanted to share his concern.

She wanted to know about the things and people that mattered to him.

"Adam," she asked him softly, "tell me about Jennifer. What's she like?"

He glanced at her, his gray eyes wary. He was distrustful of her sudden interest in Jennifer, as if she were using his daughter to insert herself in his life.

"Why do you want to know about Jenny?" he asked her suspiciously.

"Because I know you're worried, and I thought it might help to talk about her. That is what's bothering you, isn't it?"

He was being unfair to her, Adam realized, a paranoid jerk. All she was doing was trying to help him, and here he was mentally accusing her of trying to make some claim on him. "Yeah," he said, snatching at an excuse for his difficult mood, "I am worried about her."

Squeezing back his reluctance, he made the effort to discuss his daughter between mouthfuls of oatmeal. "I don't know. I guess Jenny's pretty much of a normal kid. Bright and eager, chatters without ever coming up for air. She likes soccer and gymnastics, and she and her friends are forever discussing this series of books they're always reading. Something about babysitters."

"The Babysitters Club," Regan said. "They're enormously popular with girls her age."

"Anyway," he went on, "I've always been proud of her. That mess about the separation and divorce wasn't easy on her, of course, but she handled it pretty well. Only now..."

Regan nodded understandingly. "Her mother's death, you mean."

"Well," he admitted, "to give Valerie her due, she wasn't a bad mother really. Maybe she and Jenny weren't as close as they might have been. Still, it hit her awfully hard when Valerie died the way she did. Kids talk, and I worry about what she might have heard."

"Especially about your alleged involvement in her mother's death," Regan said. "That's it, isn't it?"

He said nothing, but the bleakness on his lowered face was answer enough.

Regan leaned toward him earnestly. "Then that's all the more reason for seeing you vindicated. Adam, we have to do what I wanted to suggest to you last night. You wouldn't listen then, but you've got to listen now."

His head came up sharply. "What are you talking about?"

"The time is running out. Any day now the ice could be gone, and that means we'll be on our way out of here. We have to plan a course of action. We have to be ready." This time she didn't hesitate. She reached across the table, covering his hand lovingly with her own as she pleaded with him. "If the oil rigger isn't in Frazer Inlet and never was there, then we have to find out where he did go."

"*We,*" he said with rising impatience. "You keep talking *we*. I told you, I don't want you involved in this manhunt."

"But I have to be," she insisted. "If the worst should happen and they arrest you again, you won't be able to go on looking for him, but I'll still be free."

"And what do you think you could possibly do on your own?" he growled, his eyes a cold silver.

They were hurtful words that tapped into her old insecurity. Words that implied she was a useless wimp. But she didn't want to believe that he meant them in this way. "Maybe a lot," she said quietly. "I'm not wanted by the law. As far as anyone need know, I'm a disinterested party. I can go on looking, I can ask questions. I can contact people willing to help us. There must be people who aren't ready to believe the worst about you, who would—"

"You're talking crazy!" He cut her off savagely. He jerked his hand away from hers, almost upsetting his bowl of oatmeal. "This isn't some third-grade game, Regan! This guy is a killer, dangerous! He learns somebody is on his trail, he's apt to pull something desperate!"

"Adam, I wouldn't do anything to put myself at risk. I'm not a fool."

His eyes narrowed mutinously. "I'm not going to discuss this, Regan. I'm telling you flat out, I don't want you to have any connection with this business. It's not your fight."

"That's funny," she said softly. "I thought last night entitled me to be very much a part of your fight."

"Last night has nothing to do with this." He flung the words at her angrily. "Last night was a—" He stopped himself, shoving aside his breakfast with a violent gesture.

"What?" she whispered, her heart sinking. "A mistake?"

He didn't answer her. He didn't look at her. Sunlight was still streaming across the table where they sat, but it no longer felt cheerful.

He doesn't mean it, Regan told herself quickly, striving not to lose her precious conviction that last night meant as much to him as it did to her. He has to care. I *know* he cares. It's just that he's worried about me. He's worried about my safety.

"Adam," she said gently, trying again to reach him, to make excuses for him, "I understand what you're going through. It's the strain of this endless waiting and wondering. I know how wild it must be making you. You're frustrated because you need to get out of here and get on with your search."

His gaze lifted and met hers. "What I need to get away from—" he stung her bitterly "—is *you* and what you're doing to me!"

He had been cruel. Intentionally cruel. He saw the pain his words had inflicted on her face, and he hated himself for hurting her. He wanted to go to her, put his arms around her, tell her he hadn't meant it. But he couldn't be soft about this. If he relented now, he would be sentencing her to a much worse anguish when the final separation came. Much better then to keep her at a distance. Oh, damn it to hell, why had he ever allowed last night to happen?

Regan pushed back from the table and got slowly to her feet. "That's no problem," she informed him rigidly, managing to keep her voice steady, though her hands were trembling. "I'll be happy to oblige you by removing myself."

She crossed the room, flipped her coat off a wall hook and disappeared through the swing door. Seconds later he heard the front door banging behind her.

Adam went on sitting there in a welter of misery and guilt. He looked at the breakfast she had so lovingly prepared, which neither of them had been able to choke down, and he despised himself. Not because he had deliberately raised this unhappy barrier between them. He was still convinced that, for her own sake, he was doing the right thing. But the suspicions he had entertained about her motives were mean and inexcusable, even if he hadn't voiced them. He *was* an insufferable bastard to ever consider that her offer to help him was meant to trap him into a commitment. She had asked for nothing but the right to stand by him, to support him out of her selfless love, and he had treated her shamelessly.

He should have handled it with some degree of sensitivity. He should have explained to her kindly why they couldn't be together, why last night had been wrong. He ought to go to her now and apologize and then reason with her. But he didn't, because he knew Regan would refuse that kind of argument. Only this way, with cold rancor, could he maintain the necessary barrier between them. But it was killing him.

He tried to drink the rest of his coffee, but it was cold now. He also tried not to think about her, but a fresh concern was already stealing into his mind. She had taken her coat and left the lodge. What was she doing out there? Where had she gone?

Oh, hell, forget it. She was her own woman. She could take care of herself.

He shifted restlessly on the hard wooden chair, forbidding himself to worry about her, telling himself she wasn't really his responsibility and never had been.

But he couldn't shake the thought that she was upset and out there alone. Would she wander off and lose her way back? Get into some mess and not be able to help herself? Damn fool woman! Anything could happen!

He refused to go after her. He told himself when he got up from the table and went into the lounge that all he was going to do was check on her from the front windows, satisfy himself that she was still in sight. But he couldn't spot her from any of the windows.

Cursing under his breath, more at his own weakness than anything else, he got into his coat and went out onto the porch. He still had no intention of following her. It was just that the porch offered him a better view. He stood at the railing and scanned the clearing. She was nowhere to be seen, though he thought he detected fresh tracks in the snow disappearing over the brow of the hill in the direction of the lake. Where was she, anyway?

He didn't try to fool himself this time as he left the porch and followed the tracks down the slope. He had to find her. He had to know whether she was safe.

He couldn't help noticing that the snow was soft and settling underfoot, that the heavy white loads on the conifers had begun to slide to the ground. The spring thaw was very near, but it didn't excite him as it should have.

He discovered her as he came past the grove of thick spruce. She was standing on the shore near the boat house, gazing out over the expanse of frozen lake. The sun on her uncovered head made her hair as bright as a new penny. She was slim and lovely, but there was a mournful aloneness about her that wrenched at him powerfully.

There was no way he could turn around and go back to the house, no way he could stop himself from joining her. It wasn't wise, but he couldn't bear her unhappiness any longer. Or his own.

She heard his step behind her and turned to face him. Her nose was pink, her eyes stained with tears. Oh, God, she'd been crying! He couldn't stand this!

He didn't hesitate. He went to her and took her into his arms, holding her, cherishing her. "I'm sorry," he muttered, rubbing his cheek against her hair. "I'm sorry I hurt you."

She had every right to resist him, to pull away resentfully, but she seemed to feel the same need to mend their anger. She drew her head back and looked at him, wiping her face with the back of her sleeve. "Maybe I was wrong, too," she said. "Maybe I was really being selfish about the whole thing."

He stared at her in disbelief. "Because you wanted to help me? What could possibly be selfish about that?"

"Don't you see, Adam? Not only do I sincerely believe in your innocence, but helping you find the oil rigger is my chance to prove to myself that I don't lack real courage."

"Sweetheart," he said gently, "why do you keep tormenting yourself about something that isn't true?"

She shook her head, unconvinced. "I don't know, but let's not fight about it anymore. Not any of it."

"No," he said, "we won't fight about it anymore."

"We'll worry about all of it when we have to," Regan said. And when that time came, she was stubbornly certain that she could find the means to persuade him to accept her help.

"We'll take it as it comes," Adam promised, and he was equally determined to do whatever it took to keep her from being involved in his nightmare.

"Then we're in agreement," she said with a satisfied smile.

He nodded with his own smile. "Yeah, agreed."

It was enough, Adam thought. For now it was enough. To be at peace and together. To take what they could from each other in the time they had left to them. It was wrong, of course, all wrong, but he could no longer help himself. He needed her, needed all she was offering if he were to find the strength to face the worst when it came.

He saw that now. He realized that she was a beautiful, nurturing woman, and it awed him that she loved him. He didn't deserve her, but he wanted her for as long as he could have her.

They went back to the house and their bed in front of the fire. Their lovemaking was slow and reverent, but with a quality about it that was almost desperate in its intensity.

Eight

Adam was still in bed when Regan released the snowshoe rabbit early the next morning. She thought about calling him for the event and then decided not to disturb him. He had spent most of yesterday afternoon splitting firewood, trying to restore the camp's supply they had used so freely. She knew he'd exhausted himself in that long session at the shed and needed to sleep. Besides, she had learned by now that, when circumstances permitted it, he was a late riser. She, on the other hand, to her family's perpetual disgust, could always be counted on to cheerfully rouse herself at first light. Oddly Regan found this difference between Adam and her endearing rather than perturbing. Evidence that opposites attract, she decided with a contented smile.

She did consider waiting to free the rabbit, but his condition when she checked on him in his box troubled her. He was very restless, refusing the tidbits of dried apple she tried to feed him. Clearly he needed to be returned to the wild. The wound didn't seem to bother him now in the least, and

she was afraid that if she kept him penned any longer he
would start to languish.

"Okay, Peter," she promised him softly, "it's time to say
goodbye."

She went and got into her coat and boots and then carried the small crate out into the yard.

"Here you go," she said, crouching on the ground and
slowly tipping the box.

There was the sound of padded paws scrabbling on the
side of the crate before the creature spilled into the snow.
For a moment he hesitated, testing the air with his twitching nose. Then he hopped forward carefully, as if experi-
menting with both his injured hip and his sudden freedom.
Regan watched him, satisfied that his wound had in no way
lamed him.

In the end, with long strides, he headed across the clearing. The last she saw of him was his fluffy tail disappearing
under the low, spreading skirts of a balsam fir.

"Good luck, Peter," she called after him gently.

She was glad for his recovery but saddened, too, by the
loss of him. His release was symbolic, like the small patch
of bare ground in the center of the yard where the steadily
climbing temperatures had melted the snow down to the
earth. They were fresh reminders of how little time was left
to them in this place.

But, she remembered, getting resolutely to her feet, she
had promised both Adam and herself that she wasn't going
to think about that. They were going to enjoy what was left
to them and not fret about any potential heartache.

In the flush of dawn Regan returned to the house. Shed-
ding her coat in the kitchen, she went into the pantry with a
lighted lamp. She investigated the shelves, intending to get
breakfast underway. Their provisions were getting on the
thin side with choices that were depressingly monotonous.
All dry and without variety. They were surviving comfortably enough on this diet and were lucky to have the stores,
but both of them longed for something fresh. Only last night

Adam had confided he'd been dreaming wistfully of a sizzling Texas steak. She had bopped him playfully on the head for daring to mention it.

"Looks like oatmeal again," she muttered aloud, and was reaching for the can when inspiration struck.

Fish. Fresh fish panfried to a succulent crispness. Her mouth actually watered at the delectable image.

It wasn't that they hadn't already pursued this possibility. This was a fishing camp, after all, and presumably the lake out there had been plentifully stocked by nature. But Adam had twice tried ice fishing out in front of the boat house and had caught nothing.

However, in her boredom, Regan had been reading that fishing guide. Just last night she had come across a passage about ice fishing. And someone, maybe the owner of the lodge, had penciled a reminder to himself in the margin. *Cove at the east end.* Of course, that brief direction didn't necessarily refer to this particular lake or this season, but it was worth a try. She had meant to tell Adam about the note, but he had already drifted off to sleep.

She decided now not to tell him but to try her own luck in that spot. She wanted to surprise him, not only for the obvious reason but to demonstrate her capability. If she achieved any success on her own, it might prove to be a useful argument later on when she meant to convince him to accept her help.

She found paper and pencil in the kitchen, scribbled a quick note explaining her intention and stole into the lounge. Adam was still fast asleep when she propped the note on the mantel and slipped out of the lodge.

Regan found all she needed in the storage cabin out back—fishing line, hooks, a pocketknife and a sharp-edged hatchet. There was even the necessary can of bait that Adam had left behind. He had located a rotting log under the snow and managed to dig out a supply of white grubs. Armed with the essentials, she headed for the lake.

It was a long walk to the cove at the east end. She could have gained the area in a few minutes by crossing the lake in the middle, but she didn't know how safe that would be since there were occasional watery patches along the shore, evidence that the spring thaw was already in its first stages. That being the case, she followed the beachline and was puffing by the time she reached the cove, a pretty spot rimmed by thickets of white cedar.

She chose what she thought might be a likely place a few hundred feet offshore. This was the tricky part, going out on the ice itself, praying it was still solid enough to bear her weight.

She needn't have worried. The surface was rock hard as she ventured cautiously away from the gravel beach. Chipping out a hole with the hatchet was the tough part. The air out here was brisk, but she was sweating before she finally managed to work through a layer of very thick ice.

Sitting back on her heels after she had sufficiently widened the opening, she rested for a moment and tried to remember what her brothers had attempted to teach her about ice fishing back at the family cabin in Minnesota. But Regan hadn't been very interested in the sport and only recalled fragments of their lessons. Already she had made an error in not using an auger to bore through the ice first. However, she had her hole, she had a length of fishing line and she had the bait.

Now she faced the unpleasant task of securing a slick, fat grub on to the hook. She managed to achieve this effort with the minimum of squeamishness. Taking a deep, hopeful breath, she lowered her line into the dark, frigid waters and waited. Nothing happened.

Hmm, she thought, kneeling on the edge and peering into the hole, maybe there's something else here I'm supposed to do. Oh, right.

She remembered it then. Jigging. That's what ice fishermen called it. You were supposed to jig the line. Presumably, the action attracted the fish. That is, if any of them were down there.

Gently she began to bob the line. Within seconds, to her astonished delight, there was a sharp tug on the line as something struck the bait. She was so surprised at the strong pull that she was almost dragged headfirst into the hole. Bracing herself, she struggled to land her catch.

And in nothing flat, there it was flopping on the ice at her feet. She didn't know what she had taken. It could have been a whitefish, a lake trout or a perch. She was too excited to care. All that mattered was she had actually caught a beauty of a fish, and she had managed it all by herself. It was a thrilling experience.

In less than half an hour, she landed three more. With each one, she grew more confident about releasing the hook, stringing the catch on an extra line and rebaiting the hook.

She had four of them now, two each for Adam and her. That was enough for today. Gathering up her gear and the string of fish, she headed gleefully straight across the lake, convinced now that the ice was still sound. She didn't want to take the long way back. She couldn't wait to boast to Adam about her success. It might not exactly qualify as the tough fortitude she yearned for, but it felt just as good.

Adam was furious when he found her note on the mantel. The little idiot! Didn't she realize that ice had reached a hazardous stage? She had no business going out there on her own! What was she trying to prove anyway? He promised himself he was going to wring her neck. But first he had to get her back here in one piece.

He wasted no time getting into his clothes. Then he left the lodge and took off at a fast trot, heading for the lake. He had reached the boat house when he saw her. To his alarm, she was out in the center several hundred yards away from shore.

Cupping his hands to his mouth, he shouted at her, trying to tell her that the ice was no longer dependable and that she should head immediately for the shore. She heard him hailing her, but either she was too far away to understand his words or else she chose to ignore his warning. She continued to move straight toward him, proudly waving a string of fish in the air.

Cursing violently, he struck out from the shore to meet her. His swift strides had carried him less than half the distance when his worst fear was realized. In one second Regan was there triumphantly swinging her catch. In the next she had vanished. He realized instantly what had happened. Her excitement had made her careless. She had hit a rotten spot on the ice, and it had collapsed under her. She had gone down, and his heart went with her!

Adam started to race toward the spot, a score of sickening possibilities tumbling frenziedly through his mind. What if she didn't know how to swim? What if she had been dragged under the ice? What if the waters were too cold for her to survive them?

Oh, God, he couldn't see her! He strained his gaze on the place where she had gone in, but he couldn't see her!

And then, with vast relief, he did finally spy her head and shoulders bobbing just above the surface. "Hang on, Regan!" he yelled. "Hang on! I'm coming!"

"No!" she screamed back. "Don't! Don't come close. The ice keeps crumbling when I try to pull myself out. You'll just end up in here with me."

She was right. If he tried to reach her by going out to that weakened shelf anywhere too near her, he could end up plunging into the lake with her. Then both of them would perish. The situation called for control, not panic.

He stopped and called to her again. "Sweetheart, I've got to go back for a rope! It's the only way! Just keep treading water and try to stay calm!"

"Hurry, Adam!" she urged him. "My soaked clothes are like lead weights, and—and it's *so cold!*"

"A minute!" he promised her. "Just hold on for another minute!"

That minute felt like an hour as he turned and sped back to the boat house. Thankfully he had unlocked the place the other day when he had been checking on a craft to eventually take them out of here. Flinging open the door, he rushed inside. To his frustration, there was no available rope in sight. All the rope was back at the storage cabin, and that was too far. Here! A long pole! It was a boat hook! It would have to do!

Snatching up the boat hook, he flew back across the stretch of ice, praying that she hadn't been pulled down into the frigid depths in his absence.

No, he could see her again! She was still there! Thank God, she was still there. But her face was positively blue with the cold.

"Th-that's far enough," she cautioned him when he reached the vicinity of her trouble.

"It's all right, sweetheart," he tried to assure her. "I'm going to get you out. You're going to be okay."

Slapping the pole on the ice, he flopped down on his stomach and extended the boat hook toward her. It wasn't long enough. She couldn't reach it.

"Wait," he said.

Like a snake, he wriggled forward on his belly, creeping toward her, the pole stretched in front of him. If the ice was bad here, he hoped he was spreading his weight sufficiently over the area to keep it intact. Another few inches. There, she had it! Her hands, gloveless now, white and shaking, grabbed for the blunted hook end, clutching tightly.

"Don't let loose," he instructed. "Hang on tight, and just let me do the work."

Gripping his end of the pole, Adam braced himself and began to draw her slowly, carefully from the water. At first the ice nearest the hole refused to support her weight, breaking under her whenever he tried to drag her over the edge. But at last the lip held, and he was able to pull her onto the solid surface.

Seconds later, he had crawled with her away from the danger area. With immense relief, he folded her in a crushing embrace, not caring that her drenched clothing was soaking him.

"Don't ever, *ever* do anything like that to me again!" he told her angrily.

Admittedly Regan did feel like a fool. She had wanted to prove her capability in a challenging situation. Instead, she had ended up risking both their lives. It was discouraging.

"Adam," she gasped, struggling for breath, "do—do you think you could be mad at me later? I—I'm absolutely freezing."

She was right. In this condition she was subject to the severe effects of hypothermia. He had to get her back to the house and out of her wet things.

Without delay he rose to his feet and scooped her up into his arms. She was too weak and too cold to object to his action. She huddled against his warmth and tried to keep her teeth from chattering as he carried her swiftly across the ice and up the slope to the lodge.

Once inside, he deposited her on the sofa close to the hearth, then quickly built up the fire until it was a hot blaze. Her shaking hands fumbled at her sopping garments, trying to peel them away. He ended up stripping her to the skin himself, then wrapping her in a double layer of blankets he snatched up from their mattress.

"I'm already feeling warmer," she assured him, watching as he searched through the first-aid kit on the table.

He found the thermometer and poked it into her mouth. She tried to mumble she was going to be okay, but he glared at her and snapped out a terse, "Don't talk!"

She meekly obeyed and waited for him while he headed for the kitchen. He was back in a few minutes bearing a steaming mug of hot chocolate. She started to reach for the mug, but he held it away.

"Temperature first," he ordered, removing the thermometer from her mouth.

"Well?" she wondered as he frowned over the instrument.

"Normal," he grumbled, as though displeased that it wasn't subnormal.

She sighed gratefully and accepted the mug. The chocolate was scalding, and she had to drink it in tiny sips. But she welcomed its nourishing warmth.

Adam stood beside the fireplace, one arm draped along the mantel, and watched her. She finally became aware of his long silence. She looked up from the mug, noticing the grim expression on his mouth and a determination in his eyes that worried her.

"What?" she asked, setting the mug on the floor. "What is it?"

He didn't say anything for a minute. Then he straightened, dropping his arm from the mantel. "I've made up my mind," he informed her, his tone implacable. "I'm going back to the plane. If the radio is still operating, and there's no reason it shouldn't be, I'm going to send out a distress. Tell them just where we are so they can get a rescue plane to us right away."

She stared at him fearfully. "Adam, you can't! If they come here, you'll be arrested again!"

His broad shoulders lifted in a small shrug. "I've decided it's time I stopped running. It's probably a hopeless chase anyway. I'm better off taking my chances with the courts. And if I give myself up now, that has to count for something on my behalf."

"No!" She started to lurch up from the sofa, but the blankets tangled around her legs held her down. "Why are you doing it? It's because of me, isn't it? Because I was dumb enough to fall through the ice!"

"That's only part of it. When I was in the kitchen just now getting the chocolate from the pantry, I checked the shelves. Our food stores are getting low."

"Not that low," she argued with him on a rising note of desperation. "And, anyway, what difference does it make? If I accomplished nothing else this morning, I proved that the ice is ready to go out. And we can go out right behind it, just like you planned."

"Regan, that means nothing. It could be days yet before the river is safely navigable. I'm not waiting. I'm not going to go on risking either your life or mine. I see now just how wrong I've been to keep us here."

He was sacrificing himself. That's what it amounted to. He was sacrificing himself in order not to further endanger her. It had something to do with selfless male nobility. And it was infuriating. Senseless and infuriating.

She yanked impatiently at the blankets, dragging them away from her legs. She came to her feet then, pleading with him, arguing with him. But he would listen to none of her appeals or objections.

"There's nothing you can say that will change my mind, Regan," he told her obstinately. "I am going."

She couldn't stop him. Not here and now. But maybe on the long walk to the plane she could reason with him. Maybe then he could be dissuaded before it was too late. "All right," she said quietly. "When do you plan for us to leave?"

"*Us?*" He stared at her, the gray eyes as unrelenting as steel. "You're not going anywhere. You're going to stay right here and rest until I get back."

"But I'm fine!" she cried.

"Regan, you're not going with me. The ice on that river could be treacherous by now."

"All the more reason for both of us going. If one of us should get in trouble, the other will be there to help out."

"No," he insisted. "I can make it much faster on my own. Now that I know the route and with the snow cover way down, I can cut across the switchbacks without losing my way. The weather is no problem this time, and it's still

early. If I leave right away, I should be able to get there and
back well before sundown.''

She understood him. He was telling her that she would
only be a hindrance to him on this trip. She would slow him
down, and he would have to worry about her, just as he'd
had to be concerned about her throughout their whole ordeal. She knew he was probably right, but the realization
hurt.

She dropped back on the sofa. She was tired suddenly, no
longer able to oppose him. She loved him, but she didn't
know how to reach him. Maybe because Adam Fuller didn't
want to be reached. Not by her anyway.

He hadn't left yet, but she already felt a sense of abandonment.

Adam, trudging along the edge of the river under the
slowly climbing sun, was aware of the signs of an impend-
ing ice breakup. There was a steady wind from the south-
west, a warm Chinook wind that was already leaving bare
patches where the snow was thin. The same watery patches
that Regan had observed along the lakeshore appeared in-
termittently along the edges of the stream, perilous areas
that he was careful to avoid. From time to time he heard the
ice out in the middle of the river creaking and groaning,
preparing itself for a cataclysmic upheaval, though there
were no open stretches as yet.

Maybe Regan was right. Maybe the waters would be
completely clear in another day or so. But he didn't want to
wait. Not anymore. Not since her accident on the lake. That
had badly shaken him, much more than he had been ready
to admit either to her or himself.

But he was admitting it now, how frantic he had been at
the prospect of her drowning. He was realizing a lot of
things suddenly, mostly just how deeply he cared about her.
It had taken almost losing her to make him understand that.

This is lousy timing, Fuller, he told himself. A hell of a
moment and a hell of a place to find yourself in love.

In love?

Adam came to an abrupt halt, feeling momentarily disoriented as he stood there on the river's edge, blinking at the sun's glare and dealing with his dumfounded state. Like Regan earlier, the impact of his recognition stunned him.

Oh, Lord, he was *actually* in love with her! It must have been happening all along, and that's why he had behaved so badly. He had been terrified of the consequences, so he had refused to confront the truth. Well, he was still afraid.

He was in love with Regan MacLeod. That was a fact he could no longer deny. But it didn't change the outcome he intended. If anything, it made him more determined than ever to get her out of this whole nasty involvement. She deserved better than a man facing a prison sentence for murder. Because right now that was all he had to offer, and maybe it was all he would ever have. So he had to let her go, whatever pain it cost him. That meant keeping his love a secret from her. Otherwise, that Scottish stubbornness of hers would never permit her to leave him. But if he convinced her that he didn't share her feelings, then she would get over him and go on with her life. He had to find a way to achieve this, because that's what he wanted for her. He wanted her safe and back with her family while he went on to—well, whatever awaited him in Texas.

Adam continued along the river's shore, trying not to dwell on a future without Regan. It was too dismal to bear. But he had no choice. Somehow he had to live without her.

Minutes later he passed the derelict houseboat where they had spent the first night. He merely glanced at it without pausing. He wasn't going to let himself remember the feelings she had stirred in him that evening, the deep emotions her tantalizing nearness had begun to tap under his bitter anger. He had to learn to forget those intimate moments and all the others that had followed them, or his torment would be unendurable.

It was just past midday when he finally reached the Cessna. Considering how long their hike from here to the fishing camp had taken them, he had made the return trip in a remarkably short time.

The plane was just as they had left it, waiting on the low bank under the jack pines. He hoped the ice breakup would leave it intact. It wasn't going to fly out of here, but there was no reason why a barge couldn't carry it to safety. If not, he would somehow have to pay for the Cessna along with the supplies they had used at the lodge. But right now that was the least of his worries.

Unlatching the door, he heaved himself into the plane. He settled into the pilot's seat and reached for the radio controls, praying that there was sufficient juice in the batteries to send out his call.

There was power, but at first all he could raise was static. He went on playing with the dials, repeating his distress message into the mike. Finally, to his gratitude, he picked up a wilderness Mountie station in the vicinity of Flin Flon, the place he had been heading for when the plane went down.

The operator was startled by his identity, twice asking him for his call letters. The searchers must have thought them hopelessly lost. Adam calmly described their location at the fishing camp, offering the assurance that both of them were well but anxious to be taken out. The operator, after a brief consultation with a superior, promised him that a rescue craft would recover them as soon as possible, probably the first thing in the morning. The communication ended there.

In the silence that followed, Adam leaned back in his seat, experiencing a mixture of relief and regret. But it was done. Now all he had to do was get back to the lodge and Regan and wait. He had no illusion that a police officer wouldn't be on that rescue craft when it arrived in the morning.

Climbing from the plane, he started back along the river's edge. The sun was still high in the sky.

As he progressed downstream, he was amazed at what was taking place out on the river. In just the short time he'd spent inside the plane a remarkable metamorphosis had occurred. The ice had begun to crack and part, slowly at first and then with an increasing action that demonstrated nature's awesome energy.

Adam had heard that when spring comes to the far north country it comes with a wild rush. But hearsay hadn't prepared him for anything so swift and so spectacular.

The river was suddenly alive with a turmoil of sound and motion. As far as he could see along its twisting length, the ice was on the move, booming and thundering in a deafening cacophony. And beneath it came the leaping waters, a rushing cataract that carried the torn shards downstream. All in a matter of a few hours.

Adam didn't miss the irony in this shattering display. He had been waiting for the breakup, counting on it to provide his escape. And now it was here, and it was too late. But he wasn't sorry. Not if it ultimately meant Regan's well-being.

With the ice no longer there to offer him a solid, direct passage, he had to find a footing along the rocky riverbank, sometimes picking his way through a thick forest growth. It delayed his progress, but he still believed he could make the lodge before sundown.

And then it struck him. He was on the wrong side of the river! The plane was situated on this bank, but the lodge was along the opposite shore. There was no way he could cross back over the stream now, but maybe the ice on the lake was still holding. Otherwise, he would have to circle the whole lake, and he knew he could never manage that before nightfall.

The sun was low when, an eternity later, he neared the mouth of the river. He was in no mood for another surprise, but nature had no tolerance for his exhaustion. Rounding a bend in the stream, he stopped in fresh shock.

At this point the river narrowed unexpectedly just before flaring around the island as it emptied into the lake. All the ice that had been racing downstream had been caught in this squeeze, resulting in a massive ice jam.

Adam stood staring at the mountain of thick white slabs, feeling momentarily trapped. He thought about climbing over the tumbled pile to reach the other shore and then decided this wouldn't be wise. He could hear it straining and grinding like a beast as the pressure built behind it. It was a treacherous dam just waiting to burst and roar out over the lake. He didn't want to be caught on top of it.

He made his way around the narrows to inspect the situation below the jam. This offered a better route. He was abreast of the island now. There was a channel here to be crossed to the island and then another channel at the end of the island to the opposite shore on the lodge side of the lake. Neither channel was very wide, and they were still ice-locked. He had negotiated both of them on his way to the plane, and the route had been safe. Should he risk it again?

He glanced at the sky. The sun was sliding toward the horizon. He didn't want to be caught out here after dark.

With caution he tested the ice, edging his way toward the island. He was uncomfortably aware of that wall that was the ice jam towering menacingly just above the river's divided mouth.

He had reached the island and was starting for the other channel when, with a terrifying rumble, the pileup suddenly collapsed. The ice shove descended on the island like a giant bulldozer.

Regan, fully recovered from her plunge into the lake, kept herself busy during Adam's long absence. She tried not to think of the brief time that was left to them in this place that had come to have so much meaning for her. But, considering how she chose to occupy herself in those lonely hours, this was difficult to do.

Wanting to leave the lodge as they had found it, she scrupulously cleaned the areas they had used, putting it all back in order. The trouble was, there was a poignant memory associated with nearly everything she handled, reminding her of their imminent leave-taking.

In the afternoon, armed with pencil and paper, she made an effort to itemize all the supplies they had consumed, intending to submit a fair accounting to the fishing camp's owner. She knew Adam would agree with her about reimbursing their absent host.

Even then, she missed Adam and worried about him. As her vigil lengthened, she kept restlessly checking through the lounge windows, hoping to glimpse his familiar figure returning across the lake. The condition of the ice alarmed her. There were open stretches now on the east side where the ice, under a hard wind, was beginning to pile along the shore. The western end, the direction from which Adam would come, was still solidly closed, but she didn't know how long this would last.

As the afternoon wore on and he didn't appear, she fretted in earnest over his delay. What if something had happened to him? Would she be able to find him, help him? Had she earned enough spunk by now to meet both their needs in an emergency? She didn't know.

The sun was settling toward the forest when she got into her coat and boots and went out onto the porch. She stood at the railing and nervously scanned the lake. Except for small portions at the western end, it was all open water now. There was no sign of Adam. She feared something was wrong.

Regan didn't hesitate. She left the porch and descended to the lake. As she worked her way along the shore in the direction of the river, her anxiety increased. She didn't know what she was going to do if she didn't meet him heading toward her. It would soon be nightfall, and there was no way she could find him out here in the dark. But anything was better than useless waiting.

She reached the ice-bound channel on her side where the river emptied into the lake around the island. The lowering sun was in her eyes, and at first she didn't notice the jam just above the island. But the ice in that ominous wall was alive, fizzing and foaming with mounting volume as she neared the area.

Puzzled, she shaded her eyes against the blinding sun and, with a little gasp, discovered the jumbled menace stretched across the river. A movement out of the corner of her eye captured her attention. Swiveling her head, she saw that her prayers were answered. Adam was coming across the island toward her.

Regan waved in excitement and started to call out to him. The words hadn't left her mouth before disaster struck. Without warning, the ice dam exploded. Propelled by the waters behind it, its immense fragments slammed toward the island with the thunderous force of an avalanche. Adam was directly in its path. Heart in her throat, she watched in horror and disbelief the destruction that followed.

It was all over in a matter of seconds. In the aftermath of violence came a frightening silence. The island lay devastated. The huge ice slabs had smashed into trees, snapping and flattening them like toothpicks, crunching and uprooting everything in their path.

And Adam? Her gaze searched the island in anguish, certain he had been crushed and that his broken body lay somewhere in all that tangle of wood and ice. She wanted to go to him, but the channel had been scraped open with the blast. There was nothing but water now where there had been solid ice before.

And then, with a sob of relief, she saw him. He had survived by shielding himself behind a thick cedar, one of the few trees that had managed to withstand the onslaught. She yelled to him as he came toward her, picking his way over the remnants of ice and splintered logs.

"Adam, are you all right?"

He scrambled down to the shore just opposite her, surveying the open channel. "I would be," he called to her, "if I weren't stranded over here."

"The channel on the other side—"

"No good," he shouted. "I already looked. It's open water now, too."

"What are we going to do? How are we going to get you off of there?"

He started to unzip his coat. "It looks like I don't have a choice. I'll have to swim across."

"*No!* You can't! The waters are much too cold! You'll kill yourself trying it!"

"There's no other way."

Regan made up her mind. "Yes, there is. I'm going back to the boat house. There are canoes there. I'll come for you in one of the canoes."

She could feel his skepticism. "Do you know how to manage a canoe?"

"Yes," she assured him. "We had a canoe at the family cabin." She didn't tell him that she had never paddled a canoe by herself, that one of her brothers or sisters had always assisted her. He didn't have to know this.

She watched him as he cast a doubtful eye toward the sun beginning to slide down the treetops in the west. "Regan, we don't have much time."

"I can do it," she promised him.

Without waiting for another argument, she turned and flew back along the beach toward the fishing camp. It was her turn to rescue him, and she wasn't going to fail him.

She never knew afterward just how she accomplished it, but somehow she did. She gained the boat house, launched one of the light canoes and managed with a minimum of awkwardness to maneuver it through cakes of bobbing ice and a thickening twilight. Adam's safe recovery from the island minutes later was all the reward she needed, but his praise for her skill and her pluck when she reached him thrilled her.

Her glow faded once they were back in the lodge. He was silent through the meal they ate on trays in front of the lounge fire. He had already briefly told her of his success with the plane's radio but refused to say more about his journey. She knew he was thinking of tomorrow and what it would inevitably bring. They didn't discuss it, but she was aware of it herself, and she hated it.

They sat side by side on the sofa and watched the fire. The last fire they would have. He held her, but he didn't try to make love to her. She tried not to be disappointed, to understand that he was exhausted after the ordeals of a long day. But she feared it was more than that. She could already feel a distance in him, and she hated this, too.

Adam went to bed early, but Regan sat on by the fire, listening to the wind in the pines outside and trying to forget tomorrow. But whatever happened, she was determined not to be separated from him.

Dawn was tinting the sky when they roused themselves and got ready. Even before Adam closed the shutters on all the windows, the lodge wore a forlorn mood, a kind of finality that saddened her beyond words.

The sun was clearing the treetops when they heard the plane overhead. Pulling on their coats and gathering their few belongings, they went out onto the porch as the craft buzzed the lodge. They could see it was equipped with pontoons. It was already circling, preparing for a landing on the lake.

Adam locked the door and replaced the key in the dugout. Then, in silence and without looking back, they went together down to the shore to meet the plane.

Nine

The bustle of the airport in Winnipeg, with all its noise and human traffic, came as something of a rude shock to Regan after their isolation in the silent wilderness. Moving along the concourse with Adam and the Canadian officer who was escorting him, she found all of it intrusive and a bit unreal. Reality was still that fishing camp back on the lake.

She didn't know what Adam was feeling about their return to civilization. He had said little on the plane, scarcely looking at her. She glanced at him now as he strode silently beside her. He wore the flinty expression of a stranger. It scared her, though she made excuses for his remoteness. She told herself it was perfectly understandable, that he had to be worried about what was going to happen when they reached Houston. But she couldn't quite lose the sick apprehension tugging at her insides.

The soft-spoken policeman on the other side of Adam stopped at the end of the concourse and opened a door to a private waiting room. ''We can hide out in here until the officers from Texas arrive to collect you," he said. "There may be newspeople waiting to ambush us in the terminal. It should only be a few minutes."

Regan appreciated his thoughtfulness. They had already run the uncomfortable gauntlet of reporters in Flin Flon when they had transferred to the second plane that had brought them to Winnipeg.

Regan turned to the affable Canadian as he ushered them into the unoccupied room. "I wonder if there's a phone I can use. I'd like to call my family, even though I know they've been informed of my safety. I should talk to my school, too. I want them to understand that my class needs to be covered for an indefinite period before we board that flight for Houston."

Adam swiftly intervened before the officer could answer her. "Could you give us a couple of minutes alone together first? I need to speak privately to Ms. MacLeod."

The policeman hesitated, probably remembering that his charge had already once before escaped from the law.

"I would appreciate it," Adam urged. "I'm not going anywhere. Not this time. And it—well, involves a rather personal goodbye."

The officer, realizing there was only one exit from the small, characterless room, nodded. "I'll be just outside."

The door was still closing behind him when Regan, seized by panic, swung on Adam. "What do you mean *good-bye?*" she demanded. "I'm coming with you. That's already been decided."

He led her toward a pair of chairs beneath a window overlooking the airfield. She shook her head. She had no desire to sit down. There was the muted whine of a jet engine outside the window, but she paid no attention to it.

Adam lowered his bag and faced her, his face a frightening mask of resolve. "No, Regan," he informed her bluntly, "you are not coming with me. It ends here for us."

Her heart plummeted over the force of his words. He meant it! "Adam," she begged him, "don't do this to us!"

He went on as though she hadn't spoken, his voice without emotion. "When you make that call, I want you to tell your folks that you'll be on the next flight to Minnesota."

"I won't listen to this!" she cried. "You need me with you. I *know* you need me! Adam, we belong together. Didn't we prove that back at the lake? Isn't that what it was about?"

He drew in a slow breath and met her pleading gaze unflinchingly. "Regan, don't make this any more difficult than it already is. Try to understand and accept it. You're mistaking passion for something else. It was the situation—two people stranded together and needing each other's comfort. Okay, that's a pretty alluring business, but that's all it was. It never meant more than that."

"I don't believe you," she argued wildly. "You're only saying this because you think you need to protect me again. You have some crazy conviction that it's wrong for me to be involved with a man who may be facing a prison sentence. Well, what does that matter when two people love each other?"

"It isn't love," he insisted. "In fact, it's exactly because I *don't* love you that I want it to stop here and now. I'm not going to hurt you any further, because that much I do care about you."

"It isn't true," she whispered. "You're lying to me."

He was prepared for this. He had been carefully rehearsing the words in his mind ever since yesterday on the river. Words he didn't want to speak, the hardest he would ever have to issue, but he made himself say them. He prayed they were convincing. "You think you know me, Regan," he told her as gently as possible, "but you don't know me at all. There's something I never said when I told you about Valerie. You need to hear it now. The affairs she had—they were all my fault. She was looking for the love I couldn't give her. If she were still alive, she'd tell you so herself. I'm just not capable of loving like a woman needs to be loved.

Any woman. It isn't in me. Now do you see why I'm trying to say goodbye?''

She searched his face in desperation and saw nothing. No reluctance, no regret. No emotion whatever. It was true then. He didn't love her. He'd never said he loved her, had never once suggested it. It was all something she'd created in her own mind.

''Adam, I—''

The door opened. The uniformed officer stuck his head inside and called to him. ''The two officers from Houston are here to collect you, Fuller.''

''I'm coming.'' He picked up his bag from the floor and crossed the room. She didn't try to stop him. Not this time. At the door he turned and spoke to her one last time. ''Whatever happens, Regan, don't ever again sell yourself short. You've got a strength in you every bit as admirable as those ancestors you're always envying. You proved that at the fishing camp. Now just have the confidence to believe it.''

There was no more he could say. He didn't dare add the rest he was thinking: *Be happy, sweetheart. You deserve the best. I just wish I could be there to share it with you.*

She didn't answer him. But the stricken expression on her face told him everything. It was a look that he knew would haunt him forever.

The door closed softly behind him. She was alone in the waiting room, silent except for the thunder of a jet overhead. She felt nothing but a heavy dullness, a thick numbness that softened the worst pangs of her devastation. The real suffering, she knew, would come later when the harsh reality of her loss asserted itself without mercy.

Three days after her return to Minnesota, Regan stood on the screened porch of her small Brookline bungalow and gazed without enthusiasm at the latest project she was trying to undertake.

It was early morning, but the air was already springtime balmy. The grass in her backyard was turning a fresh green. Daffodils bloomed in a ring around the birdbath where a grosbeak was splashing happily. Weather-wise, it was exactly the right kind of day to set up her porch for the coming summer season. She remembered other years when she had eagerly removed the plastic covers from her wicker furniture, carried the flowered cushions from storage in the garage and grouped her favorite potted plants in the corners—all in anticipation of long, pleasant twilights spent in her favorite spot on the chaise longue.

But it wasn't budding trees and the smell of new-mown lawn that she longed for now. What she wanted were snow-laden evergreens and snapping log fires. That was why she surveyed the porch with little interest. She had forced herself to come out here and had made a beginning by sweeping the floor. But the false energy she had been operating on for three days suddenly failed her. Now all she did was stand there and watch the grosbeak in the birdbath.

The trouble was she didn't have enough solid, worthwhile work to occupy her. A substitute teacher was still covering her class. Her principal, wanting to be kind, had ordered her to stay home for the rest of the week, insisting that after her traumatic experience in the wilderness she needed a chance to rest and recover. Her family had agreed.

But Regan hadn't rested. She *couldn't* rest. She had spent the long days ferociously cleaning her house and laundering every garment she owned. During the even longer evenings she had graded papers for her substitute and worked up lesson plans. But none of it was enough. None of it could keep her restless mind from remembering that scene in the Winnipeg airport nor lift the resulting desolation that was similar to a fist squeezing her heart.

A wet tongue licked comfortingly at the back of her hand dangling at her side. Regan looked down to find her Irish setter pressing against her legs. The dog, sensing her unhappiness, had been as dispirited as his mistress since her return.

She smiled at him gently. "What's the matter? No worthwhile electrical cords to chew on today?" A tail waved slowly against her thigh as she tangled her fingers in his silky red coat.

"Oh, Russell," she appealed bleakly, "how do I begin forgetting him?"

The setter's answer was to flop down at her feet and look mournful.

"I know. Me, too."

She was reaching for the broom again when the front door at the other end of the house banged open, and a familiar voice hollered, "Where are you?"

"Out back," Regan called. "Come on through."

Seconds later, her sister, Dru, tall and elegant, appeared on the porch. "What are you doing out here?"

"Getting the porch ready for summer. Have a seat."

Dru viewed the dusty plastic covers with distaste. "Where?"

"Oh, sorry." Regan whipped the covers off a pair of wicker chairs. Her sister arranged her slim figure in one of them while she settled in the other facing her. "Why aren't you at work?" Dru was a buyer for one of St. Paul's better department stores. With Dru, everything had to be better, if not best.

"I had a free half day coming to me." She looked down, her carefully plucked eyebrows arching as she inspected the immaculately groomed nails on her left hand. It was one of Dru's familiar mannerisms, demonstrating an attitude of slight superiority. No one who really knew her ever minded, though. They realized that underneath was something more genuine, notably the maternal quality Regan had once described for Adam.

She had a suspicion now that she was about to be treated to Dru's true motherly nature. "And you decided to spend

it visiting me instead of The Imagemaker beauty parlor,"
Regan observed dryly.

Her sister looked up, meeting her gaze. "Let's just say
I've been elected by the family to call on you."

"Whatever for?"

Dru looked away, this time checking the nails on her right
hand. If Regan hadn't known better, she would have said
her sister was feeling awkward about their meeting. "We're
worried about you, that's why. Or haven't you noticed just
how unhappy you've been since you got back to Brookline?"

"I've noticed," Regan mumbled. "Believe me I've noticed."

There was silence on the porch except for the soft grinding of Russell's jaws. For a change, the setter was gnawing
on one of his rubber balls instead of an appliance cord.

Abruptly Dru hunched forward on the wicker chair, her
velvet-brown eyes filled with concern. "You don't mind my
interfering, do you, Reggie? It's only because I care and
want to help if I can."

Regan was astonished. Her sister had never once bothered to ask or apologize before freely imposing her advice
on her. And there was something else. Something equally
unfamiliar. Dru was actually wearing a respect in her gaze
that was just short of humility as she considered her.

"What's going on?" Regan asked. "If the family has
been so worried, then why haven't I heard about it? I
wouldn't expect Midge to tell me because she never notices
anything. But Mom or Dad would have mentioned it right
off, and the boys are never shy about putting in their two
cents worth. They always do where I'm concerned. Everybody does."

"Well—" Dru actually squirmed in her chair "—the
thing is, Reggie, we've all been kind of tiptoeing around you
since you got back. Truth is, we're a little, uh, intimidated
by the new Regan MacLeod."

Regan stared at her in disbelief. "What are you talking about?"

"It's true. You've changed. Under all that moroseness is someone we have to get to know all over again."

Regan, realizing that she was about to hear something vital about herself, leaned forward tensely in her chair. "How?" she demanded. "Changed how?"

Dru searched for the right words. "It's as if...oh, I don't know...as if just overnight you went and lost all that old insecurity about yourself. I mean, yes, you're terribly unhappy about something, we can all see that, but underneath there's this...this kind of self-assurance you never had before. You're no longer timid, Reggie."

Her sister waited for her reaction, watching her. When Regan had no answer, Dru probed gently, "What happened up there with you and that guy, Reggie? What did he do to you?"

But Regan wasn't listening to her now. She was too busy being astounded by Dru's revelation. It was true! Everything her sister said was absolutely true! She could suddenly see and accept it with a startling clarity. She *wasn't* afraid of life and its risks anymore. But then why, *why* hadn't she been able to recognize this new strength in herself until this moment? Was it because she'd been so preoccupied with her despair over Adam? No, it was more complex than that. She even thought she could begin to understand it.

The courage she had yearned for and apparently won had crept up on her, occurring not overnight and dramatically but earned in a piecemeal fashion with each new challenge in the wilderness she had met and conquered. And because it had come to her bit by bit, she had failed to acknowledge her achievement, denying its existence all over again when the next ordeal confronted her.

Adam had tried to tell her. All along he had sought to convince her that inside her was a wellspring of courage she had probably always possessed but hadn't the self-confidence to tap. Even there at the very end he had tried to tell her. Why hadn't she listened to him? Why hadn't she believed? But this wasn't so hard to understand, either.

You *didn't* always believe the man you loved and who loved you. Because you knew love *could* be blind. That he would always see the best in you, whether it was true or not.

Oh, she'd been a fool. He *did* love her then! He *had* been lying when he claimed he was incapable of love. Otherwise, he would never have been so determined to convince her to believe in herself. He simply wouldn't have cared that much! But her silly, shortsighted pride had refused to accept—

"Reggie," her sister insisted, repeating herself, "what did happen at that fishing camp? Considering the change in you, it couldn't have been all bad."

"No," Regan agreed slowly, "no, it wasn't all bad. In fact . . ."

She told Dru then. She shared it all, everything that she had been painfully keeping to herself since her return to Minnesota. When she had purged herself finally, she watched her silent and thoughtful sister and knew she was about to be predictably maternal.

"What—what do you think?" Regan anxiously asked her.

"What I think," Dru said plainly, simply, "is that you went and gave up on him too easily."

Dru was right! It *was* just that simple! She had been so caught up in feeling sorry for herself that, once again, she had let Adam protect her from himself. Well, damn it, she neither wanted nor needed his nobility. Not anymore. Not when she had her own strength to rely on now. He had wanted her to believe in herself, hadn't he? All right, she was going to do just that, and more. She was going to believe in *him* as well. All of which meant one thing: going to Texas and fighting for him with everything she had. She could do it, too, because along with her newfound courage, she had another weapon that Adam Fuller wasn't counting on.

Tenacity. The tenacity of her Scottish forefathers. And just let him try to hold out against that!

"Dru," she asked her sister with calm resolution, "would you do me a big favor?"

"What?"

"Keep Russell for me at your place? I don't think Mom and Dad could stand another long visit from him."

"You're going to Houston," Dru said.

"Just as soon as I can get a flight," Regan informed her with a smile and a stubborn gleam in her eyes.

Adam couldn't believe what he was seeing through the glass barrier that separated inmates from their visitors. When they had told him that a woman was here to see him, he had assumed it was his sister-in-law coming to plead with him again to let Jenny visit him. He didn't want his daughter in this place and finding him this way, no matter how eager she was to be with him. He'd been prepared to tell Kate that all over again.

But it wasn't his sister-in-law facing him on the other side of the glass screen. It was the woman he had expected to never lay eyes on again. And, perversely, the one woman he had ached to see.

His first reaction after shock was pleasure. She looked absolutely fantastic sitting there so matter-of-factly, her russet hair tumbling casually to her shoulders, her sherry-colored eyes smiling at him warmly. Fantastic and yet different at the same time, not the woman he had known on a wilderness lake in Canada. He thought at first it was because of her clothes. He had never seen her in anything dressy. Now she was wearing this stylish, burgundy-colored outfit that suited her provocative figure. Then he decided it couldn't be the dress. It was something inside Regan herself that made her positively radiant, a maturity and self-assurance that she had never possessed before. She had found her confidence at last, and this was the impressive result.

Adam's second reaction was a painful longing. He wanted nothing more than to hold her again. Instead, there was the soundproofed glass wall keeping them apart. His urge was to smash it down and haul her into his arms; to take her far away from this impersonal, sterile visitor's hall to a place where they could be together and alone as they had been at the fishing lodge.

His third reaction was anger that Regan should be here at all, that she had defied his express wish not to come to Houston. He didn't want her seeing him this way, locked up and helpless. He didn't want her here risking herself for him.

All of these jumbled emotions took no more time to pass through his mind than the few seconds needed to recover his initial amazement and to settle himself in the chair opposite her. In the end it was his anger, an anger based on fear of her intentions, that prevailed as he snatched up the phone on his side.

Regan had already lifted her own receiver and had it to her ear as he blasted her through the line. He didn't tell her how wonderful she looked and how much he wanted her. What he growled was a furious "What in sweet hell do you think you're doing by coming down here? I thought I made it clear back in—"

"Adam," she interrupted him serenely, "don't let's go through all that again. It's such a waste when they're allowing us only so much time."

She proceeded to overlook his rusty-voiced objection, just as she ignored the guard who observed them from a discreet distance. "Now," she went on complacently, as though he weren't glowering at her through the maddening glass, "I talked to them at the desk out front, and they were very nice. Everyone's been helpful since I got off the plane this morning and managed to go through all the channels to get here. Anyway, they explained to me how, when you were arraigned, the judge refused to release you on bail because you fled the country and that's why you have to remain here until the trial."

"Regan—"

"That's a big negative, I know. It means you can't do anything yourself about locating this oil rigger. But it's all right. I'll manage somehow, and I'm sure there are others willing to help."

"Regan, *listen* to me!"

"I am, Adam. Oh—" She made a face of sympathetic realization. "Of course, I understand. You're a man used to helping himself. I mean, even stranded as we were at the fishing lodge, you could be decisive and in control. Now you're locked up here and unable to take charge. It has to be awful for you."

"Regan, please—"

"Adam, I know you hate it, but it's no good fighting it. You simply don't have a choice about it. You're just going to have to let me take over for you."

"Damn it, you can't do this! You just can't! It's too dangerous, it's—"

"It won't be," she promised him brightly. "You can count on me not trying anything remotely risky. I'll get professionals to do that. I'll hound whoever I have to to locate that oil rigger. I can do it, Adam. I'm a survivor. Didn't we prove that about me in the wilderness? And survivors don't give up. They win."

"This is crazy," he pleaded with her wildly. "You're not talking sense. You're—"

"Determined not to be defeated," she supplied for him firmly. "Now stop fussing because I'm going to need you to do your part on this end. You'll have to concentrate and try to remember all you can about the oil rigger, any little scrap of information you learned from Valerie that you might have overlooked before. We'll want the best description possible. Oh, yes, that old fellow you bribed in the bar, the one who gave you a few more details about Valerie's Ricky—we ought to know what he looks like, too, so we can find him again. Maybe he can tell us more. A name would be good, if you can possibly come up with it, because—"

She was exasperating, infuriating in her single-minded certainty. How was he going to get through to her?

"No!" he interrupted her savagely, almost biting the mouthpiece in his seething frustration. "Go home where you belong! I don't want you interfering in my life! Damn it to hell, just go home, will you?"

"Anyway," she went on blithely, as though she never noticed he was ready to pound the glass between them, "you can have all this ready for me when I visit you again, which I will be doing just as soon as they let me."

It was useless. She wasn't going to listen to him. What on earth had happened to her? How, overnight, had she gone and lost all her timidity and replaced it with this bulldog bravery? What had he helped to create up on that ice-locked lake? Whatever it was, it was backfiring on him.

"That's about it for now," she said. "So, I should go because there are loads of people for me to see and things to be done. I just wanted you to know I'm here and working for you. Oh, is there anything you need? Anything they'll let me bring in to you?"

"No. Yes. You can answer a question for me." It was time to bring up the heavy guns, make one last massive effort to get her on the next flight back to Minnesota.

"What?" she asked carefully.

"Why are you doing this? If you think it's because I love you, you're dead wrong. I told you back in Canada I don't love you, and that hasn't changed, and it never will. Regan, listen to me—*I don't love you.*"

There was a moment of strained silence on the line. He watched her through the glass, waiting for her expression to change, hating himself but wanting her out of this and safe.

To his amazement she smiled at him, a soft, indulgent smile. "Yes, I know. That's exactly why I'm here," she said obscurely. "See you soon, darling."

"Regan, wait! Don't go—"

Too late. She had already put down the phone. She was leaving. Frantic, he watched her turn with a last little wave before she disappeared around a corner.

He wouldn't see her again, he decided as he sat brooding in his cell. He would make that very clear to the guards, and they would send her away. *Sorry, but the prisoner is refusing your visit, and he does have that right*. She'd get discouraged then and go back to Minnesota.

No! He couldn't do that! The new Regan would never give up that easily. She'd go on merrily involving herself in this whole mess and end up getting hurt. If nothing else, he had to see her in order to know what she was up to. But just one more meeting, he promised himself, and this time he would be ready for her. No more enraged outbursts. He would be calm and rational, explain to her forcefully and logically why she had to return to her classroom and forget about him.

She was back on Wednesday, and Adam knew he was in trouble the minute he was settled and facing her through the glass. She was wearing green this time, a kelly green. The dress was meant to be demure, but it managed to emphasize her tantalizing breasts. It drove him crazy. *She* drove him crazy.

He made an effort to compose himself. He picked up the phone and spoke to her. He was very reasonable about it, very practical sounding, just as he'd promised himself.

"You might as well know straight off, Regan, that I haven't done what you asked. I haven't come up with any more information about the oil rigger or that old guy in the bar. I don't know any more details, and if I did know them I wouldn't share them with you. I'd tell them to the individual I'm supposed to tell them to, my lawyer. Am I making myself clear this time?"

She shot him down immediately. With a buoyant smile, she started to plunge into a lengthy and spirited progress report. "Don't worry about that, Adam, because when I spoke to your lawyer he—"

"*What?* You had no right! *He* had no right!"

"Yes, I know, but he was very understanding and encouraging. It's all beginning to look good. He agreed that the smartest thing I could do was to hire a private investigator, which is what I went ahead and did. Your construction foreman, Hap, helped me to find one. Hap is very concerned about you. Don't worry about the cost. It's being covered, and we can work all of that out later. The important thing is, there's someone on the case, and he already has several promising leads in the bars where the oil riggers hang out."

"How?" Adam demanded. "You tell me just how those expenses are being covered! Not later, *now!*" He was losing his self-control. He could feel himself losing it. He couldn't help it.

"Oh. Well, the word sort of got around through Hap and your men, and all of your friends chipped in. Now, Adam, don't look like that. They wanted to do it. They've been sick with worry about you, and this is their way of showing they care. Do you know how many people out there care, *really* care? Well, there are lots of them, like, for instance, that old lady who lives next door to you. She told me all about it, how her arthritis sometimes made her helpless and you'd run errands for her or fix whatever was broken in her condo. People like that."

"Regan—"

"Why did you think you were alone, Adam? You were never alone. They love you because you've been good to all of them without ever asking for anything in return. You should have trusted them to believe in you. Whatever Valerie's neighbors are saying, there isn't one of your friends who think you could have killed her. Even your sister-in-law Kate is convinced you're innocent. I gather there was no love lost between her and her sister. By the way, did you know that she and Hap are interested in each other? That's how I met Hap, at her place. Anyway, my guess is Kate won't be totally career-involved for very long."

Adam stared at her in bewilderment. It was coming too thick and too fast. He couldn't take it in. "You've been with Kate?"

"Well, I had to pick up the key to your condo. I met Jennifer, of course. She's a sweetheart, Adam. Everything you said she was. I can see why you're so proud of her. I think she likes me, too."

"The key to my condo?"

"Yes, I'm staying there. Kate was sure you wouldn't mind when she offered the key. So don't be angry, because there was just no choice about it. After all, I couldn't take your dog back to my hotel room."

"Tex," he said weakly. "You and Tex—"

"Right. I got him from the kennel and brought him home. Adam, I had to. I couldn't stand the thought of his being there all this time. Think of how lonely he was without you. Now, here comes the tough part."

He watched her with mounting consternation as she finally paused to draw her first obvious breath.

"It hurts me to say it, Fuller," she went on to inform him, this time without a trace of a smile, "but you lied to me. That mutt of yours isn't capable of one single feat you boasted about that night at the lodge. I know because I tried him. Lovable, I admit, but a definite mental deficiency. So, have I forgotten anything? Yes, that battered pickup of yours. One of your neighbors complained about it being parked out front all this time. I just smiled and told him it added character to the place, but maybe we're going to have to move it."

She was in his life, like it or not. Up to her ears in his life. He couldn't stand it. He had to get a handle on the whole thing, take back control.

He leaned toward the glass, his voice tense, desperate with pleading. "Regan, you've got to hear me. You've got to stop this right now. I don't want you going after that oil rigger.

He's a killer, and if he finds out you're behind this search for him—No, damn it, don't shake your head! Listen to me! Even if you should locate him, what good is it going to do when the cops refuse to connect him with Valerie? I've finally had to accept that, and you have to accept it, too, and give up this whole crazy pursuit."

"Well, Adam," she answered him mildly, "I did give you fair warning back at the lodge that, whatever else I haven't been, I've always been obstinate. Remember? And don't worry about the police listening and believing, because I'll find a way to take care of that, too. And, Adam, you can't give up hope. You've got to have faith that the oil rigger is out there somewhere and that we're going to find him."

It was useless. She couldn't be budged. She was like a rock. A *deaf* rock. So he fought back again with the only weapon he had. Only this time around he was afraid his voice was a shade less convincing.

"Why won't you listen to me? Why won't you understand that your whole effort is pointless when I don't love you?"

"Of course," she said briskly. "You told me that last time. I didn't forget it."

"Regan—"

"We can talk about all that when you get out of here. You just concentrate on keeping up your spirit, because we're going to have you out of here in nothing flat."

She was putting down her phone. She was leaving him once more.

"Regan?"

This time he bellowed it, and the guard frowned at him warningly. Regan was paying no attention. She was on her way out of the visitor's hall.

What was he going to do about her? What *could* he do when he was locked up in here while she went on blissfully directing this dangerous manhunt, involving just about everyone she came in contact with? God, she even had the jail guards on her side. She'd made friends with all of them, and they'd offered their own varieties of sympathy and advice. The worst of it was, underneath all of his anguish he was secretly proud of her.

It wasn't pride he felt, however, when she appeared on Friday. It was a hot Texas day, and she was wearing a sundress. A simple white sundress. Nothing glamorous about it. Except it revealed acres of her tempting, sweet flesh.

He stared at her as she faced him through the glass, teased by the creamy roundness of her bare shoulders, the swell of her breasts with an arousing glimpse of cleavage at the scooped neckline, the smooth column of her throat. The hardest part was his inability to reach out and touch her. And if he *could* touch that soft neck, what would he do? Caress it with his mouth or wring it with his angry hands?

He made himself forget her pretty throat and concentrate on her face. That was when he saw the excitement shining in her eyes. She pointed eagerly to his phone.

They picked up their receivers at the same time. Her voice was a breathless rush. "We've got it, Adam! We found him! The oil rigger's name is Richard Huber, and he never went to Frazer Inlet! He went to Louisiana! He's there now working on a rig in the Gulf!"

"How?" he whispered, his voice husky and disbelieving. "How did you—"

"It wasn't me, of course. It was the private investigator. He finally found someone in one of the bars willing to talk. Not any of the other riggers. If they ever knew anything, they refused to tell him. It was a woman, and she'd been involved with this Richard Huber herself. He'd been abusive to her, just as he'd been with Valerie, so she harbored no loyalty toward him. The investigator followed up on her information, and sure enough that's where he located him. The investigator knows his business. He was smart enough not to approach our man. He's leaving that up to the police."

"The police will—"

"Well, that's the difficult part. I took the investigator's findings to the detective here who's in charge of the whole case. He's an awfully surly type, Adam. We really went around about it. I told him that if you were actually guilty and running away, you certainly wouldn't have picked a place like Frazer Inlet to hide in. And the only reason you had gone there was to follow the trail of the real murderer. Only he wasn't ready to be convinced, even when I shoved the investigator's evidence right under his nose. He accused me of being a meddler. 'Darn right I'm a meddler,' I told him. 'It's about time somebody was.' Then I asked him, 'Sergeant, do you have a wife?' 'Yeah,' he said. 'So what?' 'I'll go to her,' I promised him. 'Woman to woman. I bet she'll listen to me and understand. I bet she finds a way to get through to you.' Naturally I would never have done anything like that, because they probably would have hauled me in for harassment. But at least I proved to him just how determined I was."

"Regan," Adam begged her to come up for air. "Did he finally agree to—"

"Go after Richard Huber? Yes, I convinced him in the end. The oil rigger is going to be picked up in Louisiana for questioning. Now all we have to do is sit tight and wait, but I know you'll be exonerated. Isn't it wonderful, Adam?"

He wasn't sure. He was having trouble taking it all in. "Regan," he said slowly, "what you went and did for me after I told you how I feel—"

"Right, I remember," she cut him off with a breezy nod. "You don't love me. Really, Adam, you don't have to keep repeating it. Listen, I've got to go. I still have to talk to your lawyer about all this, and then your daughter and I have a date for hamburgers. Just hang in there and be patient. It won't be long now."

She was gone, and this time he didn't try to stop her. He was still in a state of shock.

Adam didn't see her anymore until Monday. No weekend was ever so brutally long. He spent it punishing himself with worry, in truth more about Regan than about the possibility of his release. He didn't know why he should be worried about her now. At this point, with the police back on the case, she had to be safe. Except he was in here, and she was out there still running around, and if something did happen he couldn't take care of her. Take care of her? No, he wasn't going to let himself speculate too far in that direction. He was afraid of where it might take him. It was too soon to count on anything.

Regan was there on Monday, and for once he didn't notice what she was wearing. How could he when his mind was still in a turmoil? All he could see was her face, and it was glowing with elation.

But he didn't dare trust what that glow meant until they had picked up their phones, and she told him triumphantly, "We did it!"

"The oil rigger—"

"They not only have him in custody, but he's confessed to the whole thing. He panicked when they approached him and tried to run. Then when they caught him he just sort of went to pieces and told them everything. It happened like you figured. Valerie was pressuring him. She turned hysterical when he tried to walk out on her. He went wild over that and ended up killing her. You're cleared now, Adam! Isn't that marvelous?"

He felt weak with relief, and he wasn't sure the relief was for his own well-being or hers. "Free? I'm actually going to be free?"

"Your lawyer is working on the details of your release right now," she guaranteed. "He'll have you out first thing in the morning."

"Regan," he said, his voice husky with emotion, "how can I begin to tell you—"

But she wasn't going to let him express his gratitude. She was already interrupting him with a lively, "Guess what? Jenny told me over hamburgers and sodas that she wants to be a teacher herself someday. Adam, we had the best time together! Oh, I should apologize. I never asked your permission to take her out. But Kate said it would be all right, so I hope you don't mind.''

And why should he mind when, the way Regan MacLeod was making everything happen all at once, he had no more say in his life anyway? But, he promised himself gleefully, the minute he got out of here... The prospect suddenly opened up a world of possibilities too intoxicating to his starved senses to even begin contemplating.

''Listen,'' he said eagerly, ''you are going to be right here when I get out, aren't you, because—''

''Adam, I've got to run.'' She was doing it again, cutting him off in midsentence. ''Practically no one knows the good news yet, and I've got to get around and share it with all of them.''

''Regan, hold on—''

''See you soon.''

''Regan, please—''

Damn! She already had the phone down and was abruptly on her way. And that's when he did notice one thing she was wearing as she vanished around the corner in a swirl of skirts. Her sensational legs were clad in a sexy dark hose. He couldn't wait for tomorrow.

Ten

They were all waiting to greet him when Adam emerged from the county jail in the company of his lawyer. As he stood there on the walk under the welcome morning sun, they surrounded him on all sides, noisy with their joyful congratulations.

His daughter flung herself on him, squealing with excitement. A tearful Kate embraced him. His gruff-voiced foreman, Hap, swept him into a bear hug. There were handshakes from members of his construction crew, questions from reporters.

With his arm still around Jennifer, he eagerly searched the crowd pressing in on him. He couldn't find her. Everyone had come. Jenny had even brought his dog, who was pawing at him happily. But Regan wasn't there. He didn't see her beloved face anywhere in that small sea of bobbing heads. Where the hell was she?

Puzzled, worried, Adam turned to his sister-in-law. "Where is she?" he demanded.

Kate and Hap exchanged uneasy glances.

"Tell me," he insisted.

It was his daughter who told him, gazing up at him with his own gray eyes wide and curious in her pretty face. "She's gone, Daddy! Regan went back to Minnesota!"

Adam turned, frowning at his sister-in-law. "What's going on?"

Kate shook her head. "I don't know, Adam. She just thanked us and left. She caught an early flight, and that's all I can tell you. I was hoping maybe you would understand it."

He didn't understand it. He didn't understand it at all. Damn it, she belonged to him! Now that it was safe for them to be together, she belonged to him! So why wasn't she here to hear that? Why had she suddenly run away when she had finally achieved the freedom for him that she had been fighting for? What kind of game was she playing with him now? It just didn't make sense. Unless...

Dear God, he'd been telling her since Winnipeg that he didn't love her! She had never listened to that lie, but she must have actually believed it in the end. It was the only explanation he could think of.

He had to find her! He had to go to her and convince her that she meant everything to him! And if she refused to hear him... Well, she'd better listen to him, that's all! Because she wasn't going to get away from him! Not this time! He'd pin her sweet little hide to the barn door before she tried it!

He was in a state of simmering outrage when his sister-in-law and Hap put him on an afternoon flight for Minneapolis. His plane was just lifting off the runway when Kate found a phone near the boarding gate and called Brookline, Minnesota.

"Get ready for him," she reported ominously. "He's on his way."

"How did he take it?" Regan asked.

"Like a Texas thunderstorm and, honey, they can be awfully mean."

"Thanks, Kate. I'll take it from here."
"Good luck."

Adam's fury didn't lessen by any degree on the long flight
to Minnesota. Not when he remembered that Regan had left
Houston without an explanation, without so much as a single word of goodbye. He didn't deserve this kind of treat-
ment. All right, maybe he did. He hadn't exactly been loving
to her since Canada. But that didn't entitle her to walk out
on him before he even had a chance to thank her. He still
didn't understand it.

He was roaring mad by the time his plane landed in Minneapolis. He rented a car at the airport and followed the
signs for Brookline. His daughter had provided him with
Regan's address. The two of them had promised to write to
each other.

His anger rapidly diminished, however, when he located
Regan's street in the quiet St. Paul suburb. And when he finally drew up outside her small bungalow in the fading twilight, his temper had given way to a nervousness just short
of fear.

Maybe this was a mistake. Maybe she wasn't even here.
But there were lights on in the house, and the sporty little red
car parked in the driveway must be hers. He could make out
her initials on the license plate. He should have phoned her
first, he realized. She'd think he was some kind of lunatic.

The hell with that! he decided, climbing out of the se-
dan. There had been no warnings from her when she had
fled Houston. His determination was back in place as he
strode up the walk in the dwindling twilight. But underneath he was actually scared by what he might learn in that
house.

The spring weather here was unusually mild, and when he
came up on the front steps he found the inner door standing open to allow air through the screen door. He could see
into the living room, but there was no one there. He pressed
the bell at the side and heard it chime somewhere inside.

She was at the back of the house. He heard her call out a cheerful, "Come on in. I'm in the kitchen. The potatoes are at a crucial stage, so I can't leave them."

Adam hesitated. She was expecting someone. She didn't know it was him. He had no right to enter without announcing himself. But if she realized who it was, she might not invite him into the house. He wasn't going to risk it. He opened the screen door, passed through the living room and a short hallway, and found himself standing in the kitchen doorway.

Her back was to him. She was at the wall oven checking on a dish of twice-baked potatoes. She didn't turn, but she sensed he was behind her.

"Hi," she greeted him without looking up. "I think this is turning out to be a miracle of timing, don't you?"

She still didn't realize who was there. He didn't know how to tell her without startling her. Damn it, she had no business casually inviting people into her house without checking first. And leaving her door wide open that way for any goofball to wander in.

He moved a few steps into the kitchen itself, and that's when he began to understand the scene. The room was pleasant with the savory aromas of a special dinner in the making. Apple cobbler for one, unless he missed his guess. And through the door that stood open to a screened porch he could see a spring bouquet on a table and candles inside hurricane globes. There were also two place settings of good china and music playing softly from a tape player on a smaller wrought-iron table.

It was clearly a romantic situation, and he didn't like it. He didn't like it one bit.

Regan turned away from the oven then, and he noticed how she was dressed. This, too, was special. Something silky and full-skirted. A dark blue that enhanced her russet hair. She had more colors in her wardrobe than a rainbow. Her house was alive with color, too. His mind had already registered that on a subliminal level.

Her face was flushed, maybe from the heat of the oven or from her sudden discovery that he was standing there in her kitchen. Either way, the flush became her. In fact, he had never seen her more lovely, and it maddened him to think she might be looking like this for some other man.

She must be astonished to find him here dropping in out of nowhere. He didn't care. He wasn't going to be gentle about this, not with a sudden jealousy burning inside him.

"What's going on?" he growled. "Just who are you expecting here tonight?"

Her eyes widened over his scowl, the only sign that she was surprised in any way. "You, of course," she said calmly, stripping off her oven mitt. "And how was your flight?"

"Don't lie to me. You didn't even know I was coming."

"Oh, yes, I did. Kate phoned me right after she and Hap put you on the plane. Excuse me."

She brushed past him, so near that he was aroused by the scent she was wearing: a subtle, fresh fragrance that made him want to grab her and crush her in a powerful embrace. He resisted the urge and watched her as she opened the refrigerator and removed a bottle of chilled wine. He was immensely confused.

"Regan, what's this all about? I want some answers."

She closed the refrigerator door, bottle in hand, and smiled at him confidently. "Later, because dinner's almost ready. You don't know the trouble I went to to coordinate this meal, including calling the airline to be sure your flight was on time and then estimating how long it would take you to drive here from the airport."

She passed him again. Still disbelieving, he watched her go out on the porch and place the wine on the table. For the first time he paid attention to the music on the tape player. Nat King Cole. "The Very Thought of You." The song called up a memory of them dancing together on another porch. A scene he would never forget.

It was true then. This party *was* for him. But it didn't explain anything.

She started back into the kitchen. He wasn't going to let her get by him this time. He wasn't going to wait for those answers. He trapped her against the wall, making a cage with his arms extended on either side of her.

"Now," he demanded. "Not later. Why did you run out on me?"

Regan was suddenly aware of his provocative closeness as he leaned toward her, his face hard with purpose. She was caught between his strongly corded forearms stretched into fists that were planted against the wall where she was flattened. It was a familiar, sexy pose—an insistent male staking out his territory. A kind of primal thing boys learned in high school hallways when they pinned their girls against lockers.

He wasn't touching her, but his potent nearness had the effect of an embrace. Regan knew she ought to do the usual thing girls did in high school hallways. Laugh at him teasingly and duck under his arm. But she wasn't sure she wanted to escape. The marvelous gray eyes were still challenging her.

"Now, Adam, I didn't run out on you. It's—well, just that I wanted our reunion to be here."

"Why?"

"Look, there isn't time for this now. I don't want my dinner burning. I'll tell you after we eat."

But he didn't let her go. He continued to hold her there. It was Russell who saved her in the end. The Irish setter had been out in the backyard investigating a suspicious chipmunk hole. And, since it was too early in the season to worry about insects, Regan had left the screen door on the porch propped open for him. He came streaking into the kitchen, leaping into the air and landing in the vicinity of Adam's backside.

"What the—" Adam whirled around to find a shaggy red menace attached to him.

Regan laughed. "It's all right. He wouldn't hurt a fly. He just wants you to pay attention to him."

The animal was all wiggles and licks and whines and wouldn't be pacified until Adam crouched down and fondled his floppy ears. Something struck him then, and he gazed up at Regan in wonder. "You don't live in darkness. There are lights in the house."

"What?"

"The monster here who chews electrical cords," he drawled. "I'm surprised anything in the place works."

"I manage to keep ahead of him. Just."

Russell, satisfied, bounded away into the yard again. The chipmunk hole was, after all, more important than the new arrival in the house. Regan exhaled softly in relief. Russell had succeeded in distracting Adam. She meant to keep him distracted.

"Here." She thrust a corkscrew at him as he got to his feet. "Go sit down and open the wine. We'll talk later, I promise."

He hesitated, and she thought he was about to object again. But it wasn't that. "Regan," he said, eyeing her clothes, "I'm not dressed for wine and candles and soft music."

"Don't worry. Half of us is. Go."

He went out to the porch and settled himself at the table. She busied herself with the dinner. Then she made the mistake of pausing and glancing through the doorway to check on his progress with the wine. No, he wasn't wearing a suit and tie. This was much worse. She went positively limp at the sight of him.

His back was to her. He was sitting very erect on the chair so that she could appreciate the breadth of his shoulders in a cream-colored oxford-cloth shirt. The soft material was stretched across his muscular back, the sleeves of the shirt rolled back over his hair-darkened forearms. Through the open mesh of the chair, she could see his tight buttocks encased in faded jeans. His well-defined thighs were spread in order to permit his legs and feet, clad in scuffed running shoes, to hook back around the chair legs. Again, it was an unconsciously sexy, totally masculine position.

Regan, breathless, forced her attention back to her salad-mixing. She prayed that this whole thing tonight was going to work.

The candle flames fluttered inside their globes while Nat King Cole's velvet voice serenaded them with his magic. The dinner was perfect. A fresh, crisp salad, cheesy twice-baked potatoes, the tender, sizzling steak they had both dreamed about back at the fishing camp. It was all wonderful, and Adam wasn't enjoying a bit of it. He ate everything she served him, complimented her on each dish, but it could have been sawdust he was putting into his mouth. How could he enjoy any of it, even the apple cobbler, which was his favorite, when he was going out of his mind with worry? She hadn't told him anything yet. For all he knew, this could be the legendary last meal they served a traitor before they executed him at sunrise. Maybe that was Regan's motive. Maybe she was feeding him before she shot him down. He couldn't take it.

In the end he pushed aside his half-eaten cobbler and surged to his feet. "The hell with this!" he grumbled.

Regan looked up from her end of the table. "What's wrong? Don't you like it? Jenny said it was your favorite dessert."

He didn't answer her. He went to the wrought-iron table and rewound the tape on the player until he located the selection he was looking for. Satisfied, he came back to the larger table and stood over her.

"Up," he ordered.

Regan didn't argue with him. She put down her napkin and came slowly to her feet. The sweet strains of "The Very Thought of You" drifted again across the porch as she faced him. She understood his intention.

Maybe this way he could finally get some answers, he thought. If not, he would at least have the satisfaction of holding her in his arms again.

They danced in the soft evening air just as they had danced on another open porch, moving slowly, smoothly to the rhythm of the song. They danced, and she felt so good nestled against him, so right that he could barely keep his mind on his objective.

"Why?" he whispered against her ear. "Why did you run away? Why wouldn't you let me thank you back in Houston?"

"It wasn't necessary," she said simply. "I knew underneath what you were feeling about my helping you. Anyway, it's what you do for someone you love."

His arms tightened around her in relief. He had been afraid that maybe she had stopped loving him, that his constant anger with her had eroded and destroyed her love.

"I understood your gratitude," she went on, "but—"

"What?" he prompted. "Tell me."

He could feel her nervousness now. "Adam, it wasn't gratitude that brought you here, was it? I couldn't stand it if it was just that."

His cheek caressed her fragrant hair. "No," he said, his voice deep with emotion. "I came because I love you. Have loved you since that morning I almost lost you through the ice. Or maybe it was that night I told you about Valerie. Or that day you rescued the snowshoe rabbit. Or—well, I don't know when. I just know that it happened and that I was afraid you would be hurt because of me."

He stopped moving with her and drew his head back to look down into her face, radiant with her own relief. "But you know, don't you? You knew how I felt before I knew it."

She shook her head. "I needed to be sure, Adam. Oh, God, I needed to be sure. I thought I was, but you denied it so often, especially there at the end, that I finally began to wonder if—if maybe you weren't lying after all."

He understood it then. "And that's why you came back here. Because if I cared enough to follow you..."

"Well, it did seem necessary to prove something one way or another."

He chuckled softly. "So, it's that simple. That's the whole reason I'm here, huh?"

She made a grimace that told him how reluctant she was to admit the rest. "Yes, that's all, except..."

"Come on, out with it."

"I guess I did think that if I mattered enough for you to come after me, then it was time for you to face the ordeal of meeting my family."

"You've got it all wrong, sweetheart."

"I—I have?"

"Yeah. What it's time for, long overdue, in fact, is..."

He didn't finish that assertion. He didn't have to. His meaning was very obvious when he scooped her up into his arms with a husky-voiced, "Which way to the bedroom?"

"That way," she said weakly, pointing back toward the kitchen. "To the left off the hallway."

The possibility that she might object to this forceful action never entered her head. She was too busy being happy cradled against his solid chest, savoring his clean, masculine scent as he carried her slowly toward the bedroom.

He almost stumbled over Russell, who had returned to the house and flopped down smack in the center of the hallway floor. The setter was snoring peacefully after his exhausting explorations in the yard. Adam recovered himself and swore softly as he nudged a wall switch with his elbow to give them light. Regan giggled.

There was nothing remotely humorous about his attitude, however, after he had lowered her onto the bright patchwork quilt of the wide bed. He leaned over her, one knee propped on the edge of the bed. There was a seductive gleam in his eyes, a raspiness in his low voice.

"There's something I've been promising myself since I sat there on the other side of that damn glass screen in the Houston jail."

"What's that?" she asked, knowing exactly what it was.

"Every time you turned up there in one of those alluring outfits, I wanted to strip it off."

"Oh. Well," she reminded him, "there's no glass between us now."

"No," he agreed, "there isn't."

He proceeded then to satisfy his self-promise. He was in no hurry. He peeled away her garments one by one with a leisurely, loving care. Between the removals, his mouth lavished attention on each freshly exposed area: a kiss dropped on the vulnerable flesh above her breasts after her dress was shed; a stroke of his tongue along her thighs when her hose whispered to the floor; a sweet tugging of his mouth on her tender breasts as her bra joined her hose; his lips branding her navel and the silken nest below it when her panties, the last to go, were slowly rolled away.

By then, Regan was no longer in a mood for restraint. His long, deliberate attentions had inflamed her to a point of urgency.

"Adam," she begged, her voice raw with need. "I—I don't think I can stand another... *ohhh*... "

His mouth captured hers, silencing her pleading wail in a deep, searching kiss. She could feel his own need surging through him now as his body pressed over hers, his arousal straining against her. Patience deserted him when he finally reared back. What had been performed without haste where she was concerned was, in his own case, conducted with an eager speed as he clawed at his shirt and jeans.

Within seconds, Adam's hard, naked length was covering hers. She welcomed his aggressive strength with a small shudder of joy as he completed his body with hers, lodging deep inside her. There were no hesitations after their joining. Their long absence from each other made the ultimate fulfillment of their union too vital, too essential for any delay.

Shock waves raged through Regan as she answered his compelling thrusts with her hungry rhythms. She lost control under him and went wild, whimpering with incredible pleasure as he uttered his own low, rumbling sounds. And soon, too soon, they were crying their rapture out loud as he took her over the edge with him, tumbling them into a sweet, blinding radiance.

"You're going to marry me," he insisted. "I don't want any arguments about that. I want us to be a real family together, you and me and Jenny."

Regan had no intentions of arguing with him on the subject as he cuddled her there on the bed in the drowsy aftermath of their lovemaking, the fingers of his big hand linked tightly with hers.

"And live in Houston," she added practically, "since that's where your business is." Then, remembering something, she broke away from him and sat up. "Which means I won't be teaching third-graders in Brookline or Inuit children in Frazer Inlet. But—"

"What?"

She reached across him to the bedside table, producing a stack of pamphlets with a sheepish, "I sort of picked these up when I was in Houston."

"What are they?"

"They—well, they happen to be all about the requirements for teaching in Texas. I know," she went on hastily, "that it sounds as if it were awfully premature of me to have collected them. But, after all, Adam, I am a teacher, so naturally, I'm always interested in education in other places."

"Uh-huh, naturally. Let's see." He took the pamphlets from her, settled them under his chin and began to thumb through them. "So, you think you'll teach in Houston."

"If they'll have me." She leaned over him earnestly, her fingers stirring through the hair on his chest. "I've been thinking about it. Since I won't have the challenge of Inuit children, what about the challenge of working with disadvantaged Hispanic children? They have a lot of needs, too, and I think it would be exciting to try to meet them."

"Sounds good."

"I'll probably have to learn Spanish, though."

"You can do that," he encouraged her. "You've got the courage to do anything now."

She smiled in satisfaction. "That's right, I do."

"What's this?" Adam's head came up off the pillows. He had found a brochure at the bottom of the stack that didn't belong with the others.

This time Regan actually blushed. "Oh. How did *that* get in there?"

He examined the brochure in surprise. "It's an advertisement for Gunnerson's Fishing Camp!"

"Yes, I picked that one up at the travel bureau here. I kind of thought maybe—well, Adam, wouldn't it be fun to go back there and spend our honeymoon in one of those cabins facing the lake? We could meet Ralph Gunnerson, because we still have to settle up with him. And we could find out whether the bush pilot ever got his plane safely back."

"You've been busy."

"But wouldn't it, Adam?"

He chuckled softly. "Yes, sweetheart, it would. And while we're loafing in some boat way out on the lake, you can remind me to tell you exactly how much I love you, just in case I— Oh, hell!"

He shot up to a sitting position as Russell, awake and eager after his nap, chose that second to spring onto the bed. The animal landed on top of them.

Adam pushed aside a tail waving in his face. "I forgot about this beast here. I suppose you don't come without him."

Regan shook her head. "Afraid not. But it's all right. He'll get along nicely with your dog. Russell is very tolerant."

"Listen, is that another crack about Tex?"

"Adam, are you going to spend a lifetime being angry with me? Because if you are—"

"Hey, don't worry about it." He silenced her. "Think of the possibilities involved when we make up after every fight." His grin was positively obscene as he reached for her around the setter's wagging tail. "Just think of all those wild, *beautiful* possibilities."

Ninety seconds later Russell found himself back in the hallway. This time the bedroom door was shut firmly behind him. He didn't mind. There was a lamp cord in the living room just waiting to be pulled from its socket.

* * * * *

A CELEBRATION

OF MOTHERHOOD!

Three specially commissioned short stories from top Silhouette authors, bound together in one attractive volume. Romance and heartwarming humour blend perfectly to celebrate a special kind of love – motherhood.

THE WAY HOME	–	Linda Howard
BACKWARD GLANCE	–	Robyn Carr
SO THIS IS LOVE	–	Cheryl Reavis

Available from February 1993   Priced: £3.99

Silhouette

COMING NEXT MONTH

COURTSHIP TEXAS STYLE!
Annette Broadrick

The Callaway brothers are SONS OF TEXAS, and Cameron is the second brother to have a date with destiny...

Janine Talbot decided to have a chat with charismatic Cameron about child-rearing because her newest pupil, young Trisha Callaway, deserved some parental attention. Getting stranded at the ranch was unlucky.

· BLACK CREEK RANCH
Jackie Merritt

Drew LeBeau did not want to sell the land her parents had left their children. But her brothers had been approached by Nick Orion, a developer. She was just going to have to change Orion's mind, but how?

IT'S ONLY MAKE BELIEVE
Donna Carlisle

Stone Harrison was irresistible. He was also irritating, thoughtless, irresponsible and incapable of maintaining his interest in a woman for more than six weeks. Allison knew that when she agreed to pretend to be his fiancé, but she didn't know that she was going to fall in love...

COMING NEXT MONTH

BEST KEPT SECRETS
Anne Marie Winston

Ten years ago Devon Walker had unknowingly left Rachel Masters pregnant and alone. Now Devon was back and the chemistry was still there. Would the wisest course be to ignore it? Could they face heartbreak again?

TWO HALVES
Lass Small

Here is the story of another FABULOUS BROWN BROTHER.

Sergeant Michael Brown believed in fate. He answered a letter addressed to "any soldier" and became a hero to a class and their pretty teacher, Sara Benton. When he came home, visiting the school was top priority. . .

A MAN OF HONOR
Paula Detmer Riggs

Leigh Bradbury had to find her father and son, but the best guide wouldn't even cross the street for her. Max Kaler had tangled with Leigh before and he still bore the scars. Why should he help her now?